WAITING FOR LOVE

SPARKS IN TEXAS, BOOK 5

MARI CARR

WAITING FOR LOVE

Sparks in Texas, book 5

Can a man find two loves of a lifetime?

Macie's always been a social butterfly, but lately the resident Queen of Gossip has been feeling blue. She can't help but think she missed the love boat somewhere.

Lucky for her, widower Hank is pretty fond of her stories and her off-color jokes and everything else Macie has to offer. While all Macie knows is dating and keeping it casual and staying single, Hank isn't willing to dance to her tune. Because he wants Macie in his bed...and his life...forever.

To the brides.
Thanks for letting me check that "officiating a wedding" item off my bucket list. Marrying the two of you was truly one of the highlights of my life.
Here's to you. And love. And forever.

CHAPTER ONE

"I WANT you to go out with me," Coop said.

Macie looked out the front window and frowned in confusion. "Outside? Why? It looks like rain."

Coop shook his head. "*Out with me.* On a date."

Macie wasn't sure how to reply, but that didn't stop her mouth from opening and producing sound. "Seriously?"

Coop didn't seem offended by her stupid question. "Yeah."

She glanced around the bar, wondering if anyone could hear the exchange. Not that she cared if they could. She imagined—like her—any eavesdroppers would be floored by his request.

Hank Cooper was a regular at Sparks Barbeque. He'd come in for dinner one night shortly after his wife's death nearly a year earlier and it was as if he'd taken up residence. Which suited Macie just fine. He was a nice guy with a quick wit. Coop got her special brand of sarcasm. She liked that about him.

And it had occurred to her that—though he was frequently in the restaurant—he was watching her more closely than usual tonight. In fact, she'd felt his intent stare on her the past couple of times he'd been in. Of course, she'd probably noticed it because she'd been watching him lately as well. It was like she couldn't help it. Coop came in and for the rest of the night, half her attention was on her job, the other half on him.

"Are you sure that's what you want?"

Coop took a deep breath as his gaze remained locked with hers. She was used to this expression. People used it with her all the time. She called it the "praying for patience" look.

"I'm sure." His response was gruff. Coop didn't mince words, which seemed like an outright anomaly to her. She didn't understand how people could say so much with so few words.

Macie loved to talk, loved the sound of her own voice as she wove fantastical, far-fetched stories. Why say something in three words when she could use four thousand and eighty-seven?

Then she figured his invitation was extended merely out of boredom or loneliness. She wasn't a threat because they were friends, and it simply wasn't possible for her to be any less *his* type.

Even so...she felt compelled to warn him. He was about to open one big-ass can of worms.

"You realize pretty much every single woman in town is ready to cast her bra into the ring the second you give them the green light to go. Right now, they're all giving you space and time to mourn. If you and me go out, it's open season on Hank Cooper. Is that really what you want?"

"I don't intend to date anyone but you."

Her eyes narrowed as she looked around the room once more. "Is this a joke? Did my dad put you up to this?"

She started to call out to her father, to give him shit for joining forces with Coop to pull her leg, but Coop grabbed her hand and squeezed it before she could speak.

"It's not a joke, Macie."

His tone and expression finally managed to plow through her thick skull. He seriously wanted to date her. Once again, she didn't know what to say. So she went ahead and spoke anyway.

"Why?"

"You off now?"

She nodded. Her sister, Adele, had come in a few minutes earlier and gone to the back to put her things away. Once she returned, Macie had the evening off. She was planning to go home and masturbate while watching the wedding episode of *Outlander* for the millionth time. Jamie Fraser melted her butter.

"Get your stuff," he said as Adele stepped behind the bar.

Macie gave Adele a quick rundown of who was drinking what and then she grabbed her purse from the storage room. Coop was waiting for her by the front door of the restaurant.

She assumed he was planning to walk her to her car, though it was a completely unnecessary gesture in Maris. Crime here was rare and what little they did have was usually of a nonviolent nature, if you didn't count the arsonist her cousin, Evan, tracked down and apprehended not quite a year ago.

So she was surprised when he placed his hand on her back and led her to his truck.

"Where are we going?" she asked when he opened the passenger door for her.

"I told you. I'm taking you out."

"Now?" Despite her confusion, she let Coop help her up into the truck. It wasn't like she had much choice in the matter. The guy was damn strong and pretty good at compelling her to do things almost unintentionally.

She'd first noticed that ability of his at a barn dance out at the Mills' place a couple months ago. Her cousin's band, Ty's Collective, had been performing and she never missed a chance to catch one of their shows, as they happened too few and far between now that all the band members had "real" jobs.

She hadn't planned to step out on the floor for the slow dance because she was hot and sweaty and her feet hurt from all the crazy Texas two-stepping she'd done. But Coop had reached out a hand to her and before she knew it, she was in his arms swaying to an old George Strait song, "I Cross My Heart". And even during the dance, there had been no denying who was in control. He twisted and turned her with ease as they glided to the easy rhythm.

She hadn't told anyone, but the dance had made her horny. Like seriously horny. So much so, she'd gone straight home afterward and fired up her vibrator. Three different times throughout the night.

Then he had done the same thing at her cousin Sydney's

wedding last month. Just dragged her out to the dance floor and once again, she'd relinquished all control to him. Put herself in his oh-so-capable hands and enjoyed the ride.

Once Coop climbed behind the steering wheel and fired up his old Chevy, she turned to face him.

"Listen, Coop—"

"Buckle up."

She reached for the seat belt, but the interruption didn't distract her. "I know it's been a long time since you've been out there." She finger quoted the words *out there*. "But you can't ask a woman for a date on the night you want to take her out. It doesn't work that way."

He glanced her way briefly before turning his attention back to the road. The corners of his mouth were tipped up in a not-quite-there grin. "Why not?"

"Because women need time to get ready. Fix their hair and makeup. Shave their legs and pits. Hell, at this point, I'd just settle for a shower. You've caught me at the end of an eight-hour shift behind a bar. I smell like—"

"Whiskey."

She nodded. "Yeah. I spilled some Jim Beam on my jeans."

"I love the smell of bourbon."

Macie couldn't argue that. She adored the scent. "Oh my God. Me too. I'd bathe in the stuff if I thought Evan wouldn't give me a DUI for it."

Coop chuckled.

"But even so, I need a shower with plain old water and soap. And clean clothes."

"You smell fine."

"Okay. Again, you're missing the point. All I'm saying is you're lowering your chances of getting lucky with this technique. No woman's going to put out when she hasn't had time to prepare."

He didn't respond immediately, but Macie wasn't exactly surprised by that. Coop was a man of too few words.

"You planning to put out?" he asked at last.

She rolled her eyes. "You misinterpreted that whole conversation."

He looked at her, holding her gaze. "Not sure I did."

She blew out an exasperated breath, perfectly aware this wasn't an argument she would win tonight. "Anyway. Moving on. Where are we going?"

"My place. I'm making you dinner."

"You are?"

"Yes, Macie. I am."

"Oh. Well, that's really sweet."

She was met with more silence, so she filled it with some general observations of the houses they passed and the people who lived inside them. Once they turned onto the highway that would lead them to Coop's ranch, she began discussing her thoughts on politics, then how she thought all of Adele's songs sounded the same—as did John Mayer's, which somehow led to her feelings about the latest *Star Wars* movie. Through it all, Coop nodded, but apart from a word here or there, he didn't contribute much to the conversation.

Of course, that didn't bother Macie. Left more room for her to talk. She wrapped the conversation up when they pulled in front of his house. She'd only been to his place a few times in the past—all of them right after Coop's wife had passed away to bring him food and to visit for a bit.

She reached for her purse and opened the door, about to step out when Coop appeared, his hand reaching to help her down.

"Thanks," she said, touched by his thoughtfulness. He owned a huge truck, the kind that made you feel like you needed a stepladder to get in and out of it. With any other guy, she probably would have made some joke or given the fella shit for overcompensating for lacking in other areas, but it was clear that was not the case with Coop. He was large, powerful, and intimidating—but not in a scary way. It made sense for him to drive this truck. Hell, he'd look ridiculous driving anything else.

Coop didn't back up or give her space to walk away from the vehicle once she hit land again. Instead, he leaned closer and pressed her against the side of the truck.

His actions were so unexpected, she responded on instinct, licking her lips when there was no denying he planned to kiss her.

Macie struggled to catch her breath, to keep up with him. The past thirty minutes had been one *what the hell?* after another.

"You asked me why I wanted to go out with you."

She nodded. "Yeah. I did." And he hadn't answered.

"This is why."

Rather than offer an explanation, he kissed her, roughly, completely, thoroughly.

Macie's hands flew to his shoulders, not to push him

away, but to hold on for dear life. Good God, the man could kiss.

Coop wasn't gentle about it either. His hands cupped her cheeks as his lips forced hers apart and his tongue swept in for a taste. Macie tried to breathe through her nose, going light-headed from the lack of air. Too much more of this and Coop's tongue was going to know the inside of her mouth better than hers did.

Soon, the kiss morphed into something even more. Coop pressed his body more fully against hers, letting her feel his erection against her stomach. She wasn't a small woman. At five-eleven, she was taller than quite a few of the men in town, and she wouldn't describe herself as thin either. Her dad liked to refer to her as "sturdy," which annoyed the shit out of her, even if it was true.

However, with Hank Cooper, she felt like one of those tiny ballerinas, petite, fragile. He towered over her by at least half a foot and the man was built like a brick house. His muscles were made the old-fashioned way, not with weights at a gym, but through hard work, and he was very good at using them to move her exactly where he wanted her.

Which apparently—at this moment—was pushed up against his truck as he gave her the hottest kiss of the century.

When he finally released her lips, he only moved away a few inches, his hot breath tickling her face.

She peered up at him. He'd kissed her senseless, but not silent. "So, just to recap..."

Coop chuckled. "I want to date you because I'm attracted to you, Macie."

"Sexually?"

If he hadn't been standing so close, she would have slapped herself on the forehead. With each passing minute, she was sounding more and more like a complete idiot.

"And intellectually. Don't want you to think I'm only after you for your body."

She snorted. "Thanks for clearing that up."

He took her hand and led her toward his house. Once again, she let him lead the way, offering no resistance. She was starting to wonder what she would do if he bypassed the kitchen and dragged her straight to his bedroom. Part of her feared she'd walk right into that lion's den and drop her granny panties without question, hairy legs or not.

Fortunately, Coop didn't put her to the test. As they entered the kitchen, he pulled out a chair at the table and gestured for her to sit. She dropped down and took a few minutes to study her surroundings as Coop reached for a bottle of red wine, uncorked it, and poured two glasses.

The kitchen had a homey feel. There were vintage metal signs adorning one wall that advertised Dr. Pepper, Rice Krispies, and Armour Franks. There was a pretty green hutch against another wall and the cabinets appeared to be freshly painted—white—so the whole room was bright and cheerful.

"So you like to cook?" she asked.

He shrugged. "I like to eat."

She laughed. "Yeah. Me too. Unfortunately, I suck in the kitchen."

"I can manage simple stuff." He handed her a glass of wine. "Like spaghetti. Tonight's fare."

She thanked him for the wine. Then she took a deep

breath, the scent of his sauce smelling far too tantalizing. "It smells delicious. Did you have that sauce slow cooking all day?"

"Yep. Threw it together just before I came to the restaurant. Had it simmering since."

Which suddenly explained why he'd simply ordered a beer and not dinner upon arriving at the restaurant a couple hours earlier. Macie had thought that odd at the time because Hank was a big fan of the daily specials.

She stood up and walked over to the stove to watch him cook. He put a pot of water on to boil and stirred the sauce.

"Is that homemade sauce?"

He nodded. "Yeah. Had a pile of tomatoes in the garden I needed to use."

"Wow. That seems a little more complicated than my idea of simple spaghetti."

"Which is?" He turned to look at her, taking a sip of his own wine.

"Open a jar of Prego and dump it in the pan."

Coop opened the box of spaghetti noodles and placed them in the boiling water. He stirred as the pasta softened and then he gestured back toward the table. "That'll take a few minutes to cook."

The two of them sat together to wait, each lifting their glasses for another sip.

"Never would have pegged you for a wine guy."

He shrugged easily. "There are a lot of things you don't know about me."

She agreed with that assessment. "You can say that again. This whole damn evening has shocked the hell out of me."

He lifted his glass and tapped it against hers. "To surprises."

As always, her thoughts came falling out of her before she thought through what she was going to say. "You know I'm still fairly certain you've made a mistake here."

"Why?"

"Because I'm not your type."

He frowned. Not that the expression was all that unusual for him. It wasn't that Coop was a miserable guy. He was just really serious. She figured that attitude was only enhanced by the fact he'd spent the last few years taking care of his wife, Sharon, as she battled breast cancer and then, after she passed, mourning her death. He hadn't had a whole hell of a lot to smile about.

"My type?"

She was suffering from serious diarrhea of the mouth today. "You know. Sharon. She was calm and quiet and really nice."

"You're not nice?"

She rolled her eyes. "I'm a smartass from the word go and you know it. And the words 'calm' and 'quiet' have only ever been used in regards to me when people tell me how they *wish* I would act. Primarily my mother."

"I like listening to you talk."

Macie laughed. "If I hadn't just waited on you at the bar and known for a fact you only had one beer, I would accuse you of being dead drunk. I know I talk too much. About stupid stuff."

"It's not stupid."

Macie switched gears, bored with that line of conversation. They clearly weren't going to agree. Besides, her thoughts kept returning to what had just happened against his truck. "That was one hell of a kiss out there, Coop."

"Hank."

She frowned. "What?"

"Call me Hank."

Macie leaned back in her chair and studied his face for a moment. "Nobody calls you Hank."

He held her gaze intently. "Not what I said. I want you to."

"Why?"

"You ask more questions than a three-year-old."

She shrugged. "Only way to get answers is to ask questions."

"Good point. So I'll ask one. You want kids someday, Mace?"

Macie choked on the sip of wine she'd just taken. "Damn, Coop. Warn a girl next time before you hit her with something like that."

"Do you?"

"Well." She paused. She hadn't anticipated the conversation getting so personal, so quick, but then again, she hadn't expected to be sitting in Hank Cooper's kitchen tonight either, so what the hell. "Sure I do. I'd like to have a big family one day."

He nodded. And remained infuriatingly quiet.

"Do you want kids?" she countered. She'd always assumed he hadn't. After all, he and Sharon had never had a family and they'd been married twenty years.

"Yeah. I do."

It was on the tip of Macie's tongue to ask why he'd never had any kids with Sharon, but there was something sad in his eyes that made her hold back.

Prior to his wife's death, Macie hadn't known Coop very well. Their association had been pretty peripheral. They had lived in the same town all their lives. They knew the same people and every so often, their paths crossed, so they'd say hello, make some innocuous comment about the weather and move on.

After Sharon died, Coop began coming into Sparks Barbeque more and more often. Their conversations moved away from hello to those enjoyed by friends—gossip, jokes, affable arguments over sports and elections. Only in the last few months had their relationship shifted once again, moving from surface friends to good friends—the kind who shared confidences and slowly revealed more personal details, opening the door to who they really were, deep inside.

Macie had told him about her friend, Johnnie, about his childhood accident, his physical impairments, and his death. And Coop talked about Sharon's original diagnosis and the years of ups and downs as they'd thought her cured, only to have their relief shattered when yet another tumor appeared somewhere else.

Regardless of that, Coop had never insinuated that he was interested in her romantically, and he'd never talked about wanting kids.

The timer went off just as Macie had worked up the nerve to ask why they'd never had kids. Coop rose and returned to the stove. He pulled out a noodle and tossed it against the door of one of the top cabinets. It stuck.

"What the hell are you doing?"

He looked over his shoulder. "Checking to see if it's done."

"Couldn't you accomplish the same thing by just eating one?"

Coop ignored her question. "Top up those wineglasses while I dip this out."

She wondered if drinking more alcohol was such a good idea. She was already struggling to figure out what was going on. Besides, she was here without a car. She'd need a way to get home at some point. Regardless, she filled both of their glasses as Coop carried the plates to the table.

He resumed his seat and lifted his glass to hers. They tapped them without a toast and then began to eat.

"Wow," she said after the first bite. "You're a liar. You're a wonderful cook. This sauce is incredible."

He nodded once with a grin, clearly pleased by her compliment. They spent the next few minutes discussing what he put in his sauce and what vegetables he grew in his garden. Macie polished off her first plate, wishing she had just a bit more. Her appetite was more than healthy, but she didn't want to look like a glutton. This was her first date with Coop—was there even going to be a second?—and she figured she should at least pretend she couldn't out-eat pretty much every guy in town.

Then Coop grabbed her plate and his, taking them back to the stove to pile them up with seconds. Despite her better judgment, she fell a little bit in love with Coop when he brought the plate back to her.

"I really shouldn't," she demurred as she lifted her fork and dove back in.

Coop, God bless him, didn't roll his eyes at her.

They'd nearly cleaned their plates the second time when headlights flashed through the window and the sound of brakes interrupted them.

Coop rose and glanced out the kitchen window. Her curiosity was sparked when he muttered a quiet curse. "Give me a minute, Macie."

She waited until he left the kitchen to cross the room for her own peek outside. Janice VanMeter was climbing the stairs to the front porch.

Janice and Coop's late wife had been best friends all through school and then as adults. Macie couldn't understand why Coop would mind a visit from her. Janice, though sort of boring, was pretty nice.

Coop met her at the door, but didn't invite her in. Macie couldn't hear what they were saying, so she decided to move closer to the kitchen door. When her eavesdropping was still unsuccessful, she mentally said "to hell with it" and walked out into the foyer.

Janice saw her first and her eyes widened when Macie lifted her hand in a wave. "Hey, Janice."

"Macie." Janice's gaze traveled from her to Coop and back again. "I didn't know you were here."

Macie walked over to Coop. "Just having some spaghetti. Coop makes a killer sauce. How have you been?"

It wasn't until she moved closer that Macie began to feel like she'd made some faux pas, though she didn't have a clue why. She and Janice were friendly, and until that moment, she'd thought Coop and Janice were, too.

When she stepped beside Coop, she realized he was standing rigidly and was suddenly tense, a far cry from the relaxed guy she'd just been eating supper with.

"I'm fine," Janice replied with a smile that looked fake. "You two eat together often?"

Macie shook her head. "Oh no. Tonight's the first time."

Coop didn't reply, either verbally or nonverbally, so Macie kept going. "He surprised me with the invite."

"Well, I didn't mean to interrupt," Janice said with just enough sadness that Macie almost invited her to join them. She knew that, like Coop, Janice missed Sharon terribly. Maybe she'd been having a bad night and come looking to spend time with someone who understood and appreciated her loss.

However, Coop wrapped his arm around her back, his fingers covertly digging into her waist in a way that had her falling silent. She wasn't sure how he was able to do that, how he could convey his wishes to her without words, with mere touches, but she knew he wanted Janice to leave.

"It was nice of you to stop by," Coop said at last. "Macie and I should get back to our supper before it gets cold."

Janice seemed hesitant to leave, but then, she nodded slowly. "Sure. I'll see you around sometime then. Good night."

Macie waved. "See you later, Janice."

They both stood in silence until the other woman had started her car and driven away.

Then Coop led her back to the kitchen. They returned to

their seats, but neither of them bothered to eat anything more.

"Nice of Janice to stop by," Macie said, fishing.

Coop nodded, but added nothing more. "You finished?"

"Yeah, I am. That was really good, Coop. Thanks."

He took her plate and his to the sink, placing them in without rinsing them. When he returned, he reached out a hand to help her stand. She assumed the night was winding up. Needless to say, he threw her for a loop. Again.

"I told you to call me Hank."

There was something in his tone, something dark and demanding and—God help her—sensual, that had her feeling almost guilty. "Sorry. That's going to be a hard habit to break. Not sure I've ever heard anybody call you Hank."

"Let me hear you say it." Coop pulled her closer to him and once again, Macie licked her lips, hoping for another one of his kisses. Mercifully, they'd both eaten the spaghetti, so she wouldn't be the only one with garlic on her breath.

"Hank," she whispered.

His eyes softened and one side of his mouth tipped up in a grin. "Good girl."

He rewarded her with another of his all-consuming kisses, and it was several minutes before Macie could rouse herself from the sheer passion of it to take stock of her surroundings. When they had started kissing, they'd been standing next to the table. Now, she was across the room, her back pressed up against the wall with Coop's lips on hers and his crotch rubbing against her, leaving no question in her mind that he hadn't lied earlier.

Hank Cooper wanted her. Sexually.

And maybe intellectually, as he'd promised. Not that she gave a shit about that part at the moment.

She ran her hands around his waist, tugging his shirttail from his jeans so she could stroke his bare chest with her fingers. She discovered silk over steel and the slightest smattering of hair.

Coop's hands gripped her ass cheeks, pulling her more tightly against him.

Her head was swimming when he finally broke the kiss.

"I'm not going to fuck you tonight, Whiskey. But you *are* going to come for me."

Macie blinked, trying to make sense of his words. In her mind, they were already naked in bed and getting busy. Which was ridiculous. She didn't put out on the first date.

Not that this felt like a first date.

This was Coop...Hank...shit. It was her friend. The one who'd lost his wife a little more than a year ago.

She opened her mouth to blast him for arrogantly assuming she'd have sex with him, then maybe she'd cuss him out for denying her said sex, and move on to persuading him to change his mind about the *no fucking* part. That seemed like a hasty decision to make at a time like this.

Of course, what came out was none of that.

"Whiskey?" Since when did he have a pet name for her?

"You sure that's the part you want to question?"

She bit her lip to try to hide the big-ass grin fighting to take over her face. Macie didn't want to encourage his cockiness. She nodded, and then figured it was a wasted question because she really did reek of alcohol from that damn drink she'd spilled on herself at the bar.

"It's those pretty brown eyes of yours. Remind me of a smooth bourbon whiskey. Man could fall into them as easy as a bottle of the stuff. And believe me, he wouldn't mind spending a good long time getting drunk on them."

Dear God Almighty. Hank Cooper was a romantic. Who would have believed it? His words had her going all gooey inside.

Even so, a large part of her still couldn't believe he was talking to her like this.

She cleared her throat, searching for something nice to say back. She failed miserably. "You know, most cowboys just use darlin' or sugar."

"I've used those before. But I won't with you."

His sincerity, the seriousness in his face, had her heart beating harder. Then, her humor faded as a new anxiety surfaced. "Have you had sex with anyone since Sharon died?"

He'd hit her with the kid question, so she figured he owed her the answer to at least one personal question.

"No."

She wasn't sure if his response made her feel better or worse.

She opened her mouth to ask him "why me?" but Coop kissed her before the words could form.

When he released her, he cupped her cheek. "I can see all those questions lining up inside that busy head of yours. Put 'em away for now, Whiskey."

"But—"

"Asking and answering them won't change what's gonna happen here. Tonight, tomorrow or next week."

"It won't?"

He shook his head. "Nope."

She started to ask him what the hell was about to happen, but realized she didn't need to.

She already knew.

Macie Sparks was going to fall tits over ass for Hank Cooper.

Hell, she was halfway there already.

CHAPTER TWO

HANK LEANED down to kiss Macie again. It was the only surefire way to get the woman to shut it all off for a little while. Macie kissed like she did everything else in life—energetically, enthusiastically, and without holding a damn thing back.

It was one of the first things that had drawn him to her. After Sharon's death, he'd spent weeks walking around in a daze—going through the day without paying attention to anything. He got up, did his job, ate at the appropriate times, and went to bed. He'd become a living zombie.

Then, one night, while he was sitting at the end of the counter at Sparks Barbeque, shoveling in food he wasn't even tasting, Macie walked over, told him an off-color joke—and he laughed.

The reaction had felt rusty as hell, but good. From that point on, he'd started eating at the restaurant more often, just to listen to Macie tell stories. It was the only time during the day when he felt awake, alive.

When he pulled back, he watched as Macie's eyes fluttered open, her gaze finding him. She didn't seem quite as confused as she had a moment ago. In fact, she almost looked as if she had accepted what *he'd* come to understand these past few weeks.

She was going to be his.

That decision didn't come to him quickly or easily. He'd always figured Sharon was it for him. The only woman he'd ever love, ever want to spend forever with. That forever had been cut too fucking short, and for months he'd been pissed as hell, angry, resentful.

But eventually he figured out he had two choices. He could wallow in bitterness and die miserable and alone, cursing God for a cruel fate, or he could find a way to move on and seek some other happiness.

It was actually his foreman, Porter, who'd opened his eyes to his growing feelings for Macie. They'd been sitting at a barn dance, listening to Ty's bluegrass band, and Hank had spent the entire night watching Macie dance with all the young bucks in the county. Apparently, his scowl had gotten darker with each passing song until Porter had told him to get his head out of his ass and ask Macie to dance.

He hadn't bothered to respond or deny or pretend. Instead, he stood, crossed the room, took her hand to pull her up—even though she'd only just sat down—and tugged her out onto the floor. His cock had thickened the second he'd touched her and soaked up the sweet scent of apples in her hair. It had only been one dance, but it had proven to him that Macie was special.

Because for the first time since Sharon passed, he felt

something he'd never expected to feel again. And it wasn't the twinge in his pants. It was the twinge in his heart.

For the two months since, he'd sat at the end of that damn counter as she served drinks, combating his desire to drag her into the nearest storage closet and take her. Hard.

Tonight, he gave up the fight.

He took a couple steps away as her lust-filled gaze dulled a bit.

"Don't stop," she whispered.

"Take off your shirt, Macie. And your bra."

She sucked in a breath, hesitance written in her posture. He was going to test her limits. He knew precious little about her past affairs. Once he had decided to pursue her, he'd started digging, searching for details about her and her love life. There seemed to be no shortage of men who'd taken Macie out for a date. However, there was a distinct scarcity of guys who'd gotten a second. And when it came to her sex life, she appeared to be extremely discerning about who she took to her bed.

"Coop—"

He moved quickly, caging her against the wall. "Hank." He shouldn't push for so much, so fast, but once he'd turned the corner, once he had put his mourning away and decided to reenter the world of the living, he refused to picture any future that she wasn't a part of.

"Hank," she repeated.

"You're going to be naked for the rest of the night, Whiskey. And that's going to start now."

"Rest of the night?"

Hank wrapped his arms around her tightly. "You still stressing over that lack of shower and shaving thing?"

She nodded. "Among other things."

Hank loved how open and honest she was about what she was thinking and feeling. He never had to guess with Macie. For a man who'd spent twenty years with the same woman, he was grateful for that. He hadn't been out there in a long damn time.

"What things?" Hank should have known she'd be ready with a list.

"In addition to the stubbly legs and lingering scent of bourbon, I now have garlic breath. The elastic is shot on my panties. I haven't been naked in front of a guy in a longish time. I'm sort of pissed that you've taken sex off the table, but then I'm also relieved, so that's annoying. I'm sorry I didn't drink more wine at dinner because I'm a nervous wreck and I have this funny feeling that despite all that crap floating around in my head, you're still going to have me naked soon because I can't seem to say no to you."

She paused as she tugged away to look at him, wincing. "Shit. Strike that last part. Shouldn't have told you that."

Hank listened without interruption. Why wouldn't he? If he was patient enough, Macie usually managed to tell him everything he wanted to know without him having to ask a single thing. "Just the last part you're worried about saying?"

She appeared to replay her comments in her head and then nodded. "Yeah. Just that part."

"We'll start slower then. Take off your shirt. You can leave the bra on...for now."

Macie laughed—a full, rich sound that filled the room. "Gee. Thanks for making it so much easier for me."

Hank knew a way to make it even simpler. He gripped the hem of her Sparks Barbeque T-shirt and tugged it over her head before she had a chance to stop him. He tossed it to the floor, letting his gaze drift downwards.

He was used to seeing her in her work shirts, but on the rare occasion when they ran into each other at social events, he was treated to peeks of her cleavage. Macie wasn't shy about donning sexy blouses when she was out and about. Seeing her breasts now, showcased by her pretty pale blue bra, he'd be hard-pressed to keep his eyes above the neckline the rest of the night. She was beautifully built.

"I would give you the 'take a picture, it lasts longer' line, but knowing you, you'd probably take me up on the offer."

He glanced up, enjoying her narrowed eyes. Her pink cheeks canceled out the sarcasm he saw there. She clearly hadn't been kidding about being nervous, and in typical Macie style, she was trying to hide it with humor.

Hank tipped her face up with a finger under her chin. "You're beautiful, Whiskey."

"What about *your* shirt?"

He shook his head. "We'll get there. First..." He reached around her back and, with quick fingers, unfastened her bra, dropping it to the floor with her shirt.

Macie's hands flew up to cover herself. "Thought you said I could leave that on."

Hank grasped her hands in his and tugged them away from her body. "I lied."

Despite her nervousness, the woman had spirit. She

didn't look away as Hank gazed at her full, firm breasts. Unable to look without touching, he pressed her hands against the wall at her back. "Keep them right there."

Then he reached out to cup her breasts, loving the way they filled his hands. He kneaded them gently at first before squeezing the generous flesh more firmly. Macie's hands remained where he placed them as her eyes drifted shut and her breathing accelerated.

Hank bent forward, lifting one tit to his mouth as he sucked deeply on the nipple.

She gasped and her fingers found their way to his hair.

He started to admonish her, expecting her to push him away. Instead, her fingers tightened, gripping, holding him in place. He was long overdue for a haircut, but Sharon had always trimmed it for him. He hadn't had the energy to find someone else to do the job so he'd tried to do it himself a couple of times. That had been a disaster and he'd basically just let it go for the past few months. Now he was glad he had. He liked the way Macie used it to hold onto him.

He teased the tight nib with his teeth and her head flew back against the wall. "God!" she cried. Her response encouraged him to suck harder.

He repeated the same process on the other nipple, and then he returned to the first. Hank figured he could suck on her pretty breasts all night and still never get enough. When he lifted his head, Macie's eyes were closed.

"Look at me."

Her eyelids blinked and it appeared to take her a few seconds to find her focus.

"I'm going to take your jeans off."

She bit her lip and he grinned.

"You're not still worried about your legs not being shaved, are you?"

Macie lifted her chin haughtily. "No." God, she was the sexiest thing this side of the Mississippi. Fire and fun melded in such a way that it left a man longing to get burned. "At least, I wasn't until you mentioned it. Why aren't you losing any clothes?"

He gave her a quick kiss. "Because I like the idea of you prancing around here naked while I'm completely dressed."

"Lord of the manor fantasy?"

"Something like that," he confided.

"I don't prance."

Hank pinched her nipple, applying pressure slowly until Macie went up on her toes, squirming, wiggling. "You sure about that?"

Rather than chastise him for being a cocky bastard, Macie's hands found their way to his shoulders. "I think I want to have sex with you. Right now." Her confession was breathy, more whisper than sound.

"You think?"

She pressed her forehead against his chest. "I know I do. My body hurts, I want it so bad."

As far as invitations went, Hank wasn't sure he'd ever gotten a hotter one than that. But he wasn't going to give her what she wanted. Not tonight. If he planned to capture Macie's heart and soul—and he did—he probably needed to take it slower and easier than what he was currently doing. Introduce her to what life with him would be like without spooking her.

He reached for the button on her jeans. Macie put up no resistance as he unfastened her pants and pulled them down. She shucked her flip-flops when the denim reached her ankles and kicked the jeans away.

Hank started to do the same with her panties, but the silky material had clearly seen better days. One quick jerk and he was able to snap the elastic. Macie gasped.

"I'll buy you new panties."

"That's sort of a personal purchase. Not something you give a girl you've only gone on one date with."

Hank ran his fingers along her slit, enjoying the way Macie white-knuckled his shirt, bunching up the material. "Figure if I make you come tonight, I've earned the right to spoil you a little."

"I kind of think the orgasm *would* be the spoiling part." Despite her words, Macie pressed her legs together. Obviously she was still hesitant about what they were doing. She said it had been a long time since she'd had sex. He wondered how long. And who the last had been.

"Open your legs, Whiskey."

Her thighs parted slowly, allowing him better access. Any concerns he had about her willingness vanished when she groaned. She was so wet and so hot, he was surprised there wasn't steam rising.

"When's the last time you had a man between your legs?"

She frowned and he sensed she was distracted, trying to answer his question while he teased her clit with his thumb. "That's another personal thing."

"Answer anyway."

"Um. I don't know. Little more than a year or so."

It was on the tip of his tongue to ask her who she'd been with, but he was suddenly overwhelmed with jealousy. He didn't want to know who her past lovers had been. From now on, he intended to be the man who controlled her orgasms.

He rubbed her clit more firmly as her hips thrust toward him. Hank answered the unspoken plea, shoving two fingers deep inside her pussy.

She cried out, her inner muscles clenching against him. He curled his fingers, taking some time to find her hot buttons. Macie was as transparent as a lover as she was a friend. She let him know when he did something she liked.

"Need more," she gasped. "You. Please, Hank. I want you to fuck me. Right here. Right now." Every word she spoke seemed as if it cost her a year's worth of breath to utter. Hank was way too tempted to give her what she asked for.

But he wouldn't. Not tonight. He added a third finger to her pussy, pumping them inside her harder, deeper.

Macie's nails scored the skin on his shoulders, even through the cotton of his T-shirt. Her hips thrust toward him, seeking and grasping more stimulation, more strength. Hank didn't hold back, didn't keep himself in check. Gripping the back of her neck with his free hand, he pulled her lips to his, kissing her roughly as he fucked her with his fingers.

His tongue plunged deep into her mouth, Macie's there to meet him. They drank each other in, and he captured every single one of her whimpers and moans with his lips. He felt her body stiffen as her climax approached. He didn't let up, didn't slow down when her back arched and she fought to turn her head.

Hank held her in place as she came, jerking roughly,

crying out loudly into his mouth. Her fingers were back in his hair, and she was pulling it so hard, his scalp stung. Regardless, he didn't seek to shove her off. He enjoyed the pain. It made him feel alive, like a bear coming out of hibernation.

He had shucked off the last of his grief earlier as he sat at Macie's counter, wanting her with a need so great, he was surprised he'd managed to wait until her shift was over to push her toward his truck.

As her orgasm waned, he slowed the pulsing pace of his fingers inside her pussy and gentled the kiss.

When they parted, he found her eyes clear and focused on his face.

"I want more," she demanded. She was tenacious, he'd give her that.

Hank shook his head. "No. I told you. I'm not fucking you tonight."

"Why not?" Her tone was pure spoiled child.

"You need time to think about this. To decide if I'm what you want."

"I can answer that right now, Hank. I want you. A lot. Very, very badly."

Rather than respond, he stepped away from her. Macie was completely naked, her cheeks flushed from her orgasm, her skin glistening with a light sheen of sweat. The kitchen had been chilly when they'd first arrived, but now it felt like a sauna.

His cock was rock hard and aching, but he ignored it. He'd take care of his own needs later—with his hand. It wasn't something he was particularly looking forward to, considering how tight and hot and tempting Macie's pussy was, but he'd do it.

"You look pretty standing there."

She seemed to recall her nudity, but—brave woman—didn't attempt to cover up or hide. If anything, her back stiffened, thrusting her breasts out in a way that almost had him changing his mind about dragging her to his bedroom to have his way with her.

To strengthen his resolve, he imagined the future he longed for. Texting Macie to let her know he was coming in from the field and bidding her to strip. Walking in, hot and sweaty from a long day's work, to find her naked and waiting for him with an ice-cold beer. He'd cuddle her on his lap, playing with her as they talked about their day. Then he'd take her—on the couch, in the shower, on the kitchen table, in his king-size bed.

Most times they'd be alone, but sometimes he'd invite Porter to join them.

He wondered how Macie would feel about him sharing her with his friend. It wasn't something Hank planned to do often, but he couldn't deny the pleasure he found in watching another man bring his woman to climax.

Porter had served as his foreman for nearly two decades. A few years earlier, before Sharon fell ill again, they'd taken her to bed together a handful of times. It had actually been Sharon who'd initiated the threesome, confiding to Hank once that she often fantasized about having a ménage.

For her birthday, he and Porter had planned to surprise her. Hank hadn't been sure at first how he would feel about another man fucking his wife, and there was no question, Porter was the only man he trusted enough to share her with.

It had been Hank and Porter who'd gotten the surprise—both of them shocked by how much they'd loved it. Their original intention had been a one-night fling, but the three of them hadn't been able to resist doing it again on occasion. Sharon had enjoyed it as well, but shortly after that, the disease reappeared. It took over, her body weak and the pain too great, so they'd eschewed sex altogether.

He wanted to try it again. With Macie. Given her uninhibited responses to his touches tonight, something told him she'd love the experience as much as he and Porter would.

"Are you thinking about Sharon?"

Macie's question pulled him out of his reverie. Shit. He had been. Just not in a way he could make Macie understand.

His lack of response seemed to supply her with the answer.

She smiled compassionately. "It would be weird if you weren't. I mean, you two were married a long time. I figure it's been at least two decades since you've had sex with a woman who wasn't Sharon, right?"

He nodded, stepping closer so he could engulf her in his embrace.

She wrapped her arms around him, her voice muffled as she spoke against his chest. "Like I said before, she and I are as different as night and day. I understand if you've realized... if you think you've made a mistake in..." She paused and he pulled away, unhappy with the direction her thoughts were taking. She'd misread everything.

Hank cupped her cheeks, forced her to hold his gaze.

"Stop it. I'm not looking for a Sharon clone. I loved my wife, Macie. I always will. But people don't go through life loving just one person. I *was* thinking about her, and I'm sorry about that. But I promise you, I wasn't comparing and I wasn't feeling guilty. If anything, I'm excited—for the first time in a damn long time—about what my future holds."

"And what's that?"

"You."

CHAPTER THREE

"Well. Somebody got laid last night."

Macie glanced up from the sink behind the bar to find her friends Amanda and Brandi staring at her. She gave them a quizzical look. "What?"

"You've got that *just been fucked* glow about you," Amanda said.

Macie gave them a playful shrug, but didn't bother to wipe the shit-eating grin off her face. "A lady never tells."

"You're no lady," Brandi said. "Give us the goods."

"Goods on what?" her dad asked, coming up to stand behind her friends.

Macie rolled her eyes. "What is it with you? Bionic hearing? I've spent my whole life trying to figure out how you know exactly when to appear in hopes of getting a bit of gossip."

Dad held his hands palm up in a cocky manner. "What can I say? It's a talent. Actually, I just listen for key words and phrases. So what goods are you giving us?"

There was no way in hell Macie was discussing her sex life with her father. "There is no gossip to be had. I was just discussing my plans for their wedding ceremony."

Amanda and Brandi had asked Macie to officiate their wedding, and while that particular goal hadn't been on Macie's bucket list prior to the request, it sure as hell was after. She'd filled out the appropriate paperwork and been approved by the judge, who was her uncle, so it wasn't like that was a tough hurdle, to become a one-time-only officiate.

And ever since then, she'd been struggling to find the right words to say as she worked on writing the ceremony.

But that was a problem for another day. The wedding was still a couple months away. Today, she was too wrapped up in the lust that lingered from last night's unexpected adventure with Hank.

After he'd rocked her world in his kitchen, he'd led her to his bedroom. She thought he was going to give in to her request to fuck her, but the bastard had other plans. Instead, he had tied her hands to his headboard—holy mother of the god of hotness—and made her come again. That time with his mouth.

Then he'd untied her, tucked her close, and gone to sleep. No amount of prodding on her part could convince him to fuck her. And when she started to slip beneath the sheets, intent on giving him some of the pleasure he'd shown her, he had grabbed a fistful of her hair and threatened to spank her if she kept trying to change his mind.

Between the slight burning in her scalp and the dangerously erotic tone that told him he was dead serious about the spanking, Macie had almost come again.

It was madness. Bliss. Heaven.

Then this morning, he'd driven her back to her apartment and said goodbye with a kiss that nearly blew the top of her head off.

And that was it.

He'd said nothing about when—or if—he'd see her again. Not that she had any reason to believe they wouldn't have a second date. At least, she hoped they would. Hoped she hadn't done anything to bring him to his senses or change his mind.

Sometimes it was hard for her to judge though. After all, in typical fashion, she'd let her mouth run away with her, so who knew what Hank thought. Maybe he'd been glad to be rid of her.

Her dad scoffed at her lie. "The wedding? Chick stuff. Boring. Moving on." He walked away without another word.

Her friends laughed and shook their heads. "There's something seriously wrong with your dad," Amanda joked.

"Tell me about it."

"So enough stalling. Kiss and tell," Brandi insisted.

"Kiss and tell about what?" Macie's sister, Adele, filled the spot just vacated by their father.

Macie rubbed her temple and feigned a headache. "I'm going to find a new job. In a new town. Where no one I'm related to lives."

Adele dismissed that threat for the bullshit it was, not willing to be distracted from the matter at hand. "Who'd you kiss?"

Mercifully, Adele wasn't known for being overly observant, which meant her sister probably hadn't even realized Macie left the same time as Hank.

And while she had never been one for secrets—not with her friends, her cousins, or her sister—for some weird reason, she wanted her night with Hank to just be hers. It felt too new, too special to share.

"No one. The girls are seeing things that aren't there."

Adele looked like she wanted to press, but Ronnie Brubaker called out her name, asking if she'd refill his soda. Her sister moved on begrudgingly.

Which left four inquisitive eyes pointed in her direction.

"You're not fooling anyone," Amanda said. Clearly Macie's mum's-the-word attitude was only sparking her friends' interest more. "Are we going to have to resort to guessing?"

"You could guess all day and come up empty. There's nothing to tell. I have work to do," Macie said, still hedging. She walked to the opposite end of the counter, refilling a couple of nearly full water glasses for her new cousin-by-marriage, Chas, and his Uncle Julian.

"Hey, guys. Do you need anything else?" she asked, quickly striking up a conversation about the weather and their latest construction job so Amanda and Brandi couldn't keep up their third degree. She didn't expect her friends to give up, but she was hoping to buy enough time to figure out a story they would accept.

If she'd had a brain in her head, she would have worked a little harder at hiding her happiness. Amanda and Brandi hadn't been the first two people to remark that she'd been wearing a cat-who-ate-the-canary grin all day. It was just her luck two of her best friends would show up near the end of her shift and call her out. Another hour and she could have escaped back to her apartment with no one being any the wiser.

She'd spent the entire day replaying each minute of her night with Hank, and now she was in a state of near-painful horniness. She had every intention of spending a little one-on-one time with her vibrator the second she got home.

"We're good." Julian reached for his wallet, digging out money for the bill. She was distracted from counting out their change when the bell above the restaurant door rang.

Macie had looked up every single time a new person walked in today. And given they always did a good business, she'd lost count when she hit the hundreds. This time, she was rewarded for her persistence.

Hank walked over to the counter, his gaze locked on hers, and claimed his usual stool.

"Hey, Hank," she called out, trying to sound casual and hoping the sudden heat she felt in her face wasn't showing up as a blush. When she saw several heads pop up curiously, she realized her mistake. "Er, Coop."

She hastily poured a beer and carried it over to him.

He took the beer, and then gripped her wrist to stop her from moving away. "You had it right the first time."

She'd had a million conversations with Hank Cooper in the past year, and not once had his voice had the effect on her that it did at that moment. Her pussy clenched, her nipples tightened and she could swear some hormone-driven electrical current had her skin humming, vibrating. Lightning could have struck her smack on the head and had less effect than Hank's voice.

She leaned closer, lowering her voice. "People noticed. I thought maybe you wouldn't want—"

"Told you last night what I wanted. That hasn't changed. Call me Hank."

"All I'm saying is this place is full of busybodies—my dad at the top of that pile—and it was just one date."

Hank scowled.

She clearly wasn't saying this well. "You know how folks are around here, drooling for any little scrap of gossip. Every single time I've gone out with a guy, I've been subjected to a third degree. You don't want to have to endure that, trust me."

His expression darkened and her nerves kicked in. Which meant she just kept talking, digging the hole deeper.

"I just don't fancy everybody nosing around in my sex life."

"Your sex life," he repeated in a tone she couldn't even begin to read.

So she shrugged, wishing she were capable of keeping her stupid mouth shut sometimes. She could feel more than a few people looking at them. Probably because Hank still had an ironclad grip on her wrist and they were talking in hushed tones. Behavior like that indicated a good story, and too many of the jackasses in here salivated for gossip. "Um, yeah?"

"And how is your sex life?"

She wasn't sure if he meant overall or just in the past twenty-four hours. Because those were two completely different beasts. "Well...I guess it's...I mean..."

"You want to play games, Whiskey? Or you want to shoot straight?"

She wasn't exactly pleased to admit that when it came to guys and dating, she was an expert player. "I usually play games."

"And how's that working out for you?"

She blew out a frustrated breath. "I'm thirty-one and still single, so..." She rolled her eyes, letting her expression fill in the rest.

For the first time since he'd sat down, his expression lightened. Hell, for Hank, he almost looked happy. "I'm not interested in playing games, so I'll just come out and say it. As far as I'm concerned, you became my girlfriend the second you had that sexy-as-hell orgasm in my kitchen last night."

Chas and his uncle, who were still waiting for their change and standing right there, glanced over at Hank's comments. Macie could see their raised eyebrows with her peripheral vision. Her cousins were going to blow up her phone tonight.

If Hank noticed, he didn't give any indication as he kept talking. "We're going to keep dating, Macie. And the end goal for me is getting my ring on your finger."

Macie's mouth fell open as she fought to get air into her lungs. She tugged her hand loose, took a couple steps back, and let the counter behind her hold her up. She felt numb and light-headed and...well, still horny as fuck.

"Couldn't help but overhear." Her dad pushed Chas to the side and claimed the vacant stool next to Hank.

"Bad timing. Go away," Macie whispered, her eyes still locked on Hank's. To his credit, Hank didn't seem to give a shit that her dad had been eavesdropping. God only knew *when* her father started listening in. Knowing him, he'd honed in on every word they'd said since Macie showed her hand and called Coop "Hank." Jesus. That was only *completely* mortifying.

"I will, Mace. In a minute." Dad turned to Hank, who released her gaze and faced her father.

"TJ," Hank said. "I'm dating your daughter." Hank never minced words. Macie loved that about him. She also hated it.

"Yeah. I got that part. When did that start?"

Knowing her dad, he was probably more pissed that he'd missed the news than the fact the two of them had gone out. After all, the man had been trying to set her up in hopes of seeing her married for years. Kept talking about wanting grandkids.

"Last night."

Dad nodded, pleased. Now, instead of being the last to know, he was the first. And he knew it.

"You haven't done much dating since Sharon passed."

"Haven't dated anybody since then," Hank corrected.

Her father knew that too. Everyone in town did.

"Yeah. And you thought you'd jump back in with Macie? Gotta admit, I admire your gumption."

Macie crossed her arms. "Seriously, Dad? Just once in a while could you try not to embarrass me?"

"Not a drop of fun in that. So, you're gonna keep dating her?"

"I am. You okay with that?"

Her temper piqued. "My dad doesn't get a say in this, Coop."

"Hank," he corrected.

She threw her hands up. "I'm going to kill both of you."

"You're a bit older than her," Dad pointed out.

Hank nodded. "Eleven years by my count. Does that matter?"

Dad shook his head. "Nope. Not at all."

Several people nearby chuckled, enlightening her to the fact they'd drawn quite an audience.

"This is ridiculous," she said, leaning closer and trying to clue them in with her hushed whispers that every idiot in the place was listening. "What's next? A barter? Discussion of dowries? You gonna give him two chickens and a cow to make me his wife, Dad?"

Her father laughed loudly. "Would you be alright with just the two chickens?"

Hank grinned, but didn't pile on. At least he seemed to notice her current state of annoyance and was taking heed. Smart on his part.

"TJ—" he started.

Dad raised his hand, letting Hank off the hook. "I'm okay with you two dating, Coop. Not that my daughter needs my seal of approval. She's got an independent streak a mile wide and a mind of her own. Knowing her, my endorsement just screwed your chances. But, even so..."

They both fell silent, and Macie was struck by the feeling that there was some sort of unspoken conversation happening between her dad and her new...

Oh, what the hell...boyfriend.

"What's going on?" she asked, leaning closer. "Some sort of telepathy. Are you speaking to each other in Morse code by blinking your eyes or something? Is this what they teach the boys when they separate them from the girls in middle school gym class? Because all *I* got out of that was a lecture on what happens when you get your period."

Dad stood, slapping Hank on the back, as he looked at Macie. "About time you started dating someone with a bit of substance."

"Hey," Bruce Millhouse called out from three stools away. "I took Macie out back in October."

"We had a date last summer," Frank Tucker added.

"Like I said," Dad announced to the other men, the two who had spoken and the three others Macie counted in the room who'd taken her out on dates, "a man of substance."

"That hurts, TJ," Bruce said, though he didn't appear very put out.

Dad chuckled as he walked back to his usual table, clearly analyzing everything that had just happened with his cronies.

Macie looked at Hank. "At exactly what point did I lose control of things?"

He gave her a full-fledged smile. "The second I walked in. What time you get off?"

She glanced at her watch. "Forty-five minutes."

He nodded. "I'll wait."

Macie considered playing coy and asking him what he was waiting for, just for shits and giggles, but he'd just laid a hell of a lot of stuff on the line.

They needed to talk.

And fuck. They really needed to fuck.

"Okay."

He seemed surprised by her easy acquiescence. "No questions? No comments or complaints?"

She shook her head. "Nope."

For a moment, she thought he actually appeared disappointed.

"You want me to ask you a bunch of questions?"

He shrugged. "Might make the time pass quicker."

She laughed. "Drink your damn beer."

The time passed faster than Macie would have expected, given how badly she wanted to get out of the place. However, between pouring drinks, dealing with Amanda and Brandi's curiosity about this sudden relationship, and the sexual innuendoes Hank kept lobbing her way, she didn't have two seconds to worry about the time.

Hank, on the other hand, must have been counting the seconds. The moment the clock struck quitting time, he was up and waiting for her at the end of the counter. She handed the reins over to her sister, said goodbye to her friends and her dad, and held Hank's hand as they walked out together.

Now, like last night, he led her straight toward his vehicle.

"Another date?" she teased.

"You gonna start going on about how you need to shave your legs again?"

She shook her head. "No. I'm a quick study. Took care of everything I needed to this morning."

"Good girl."

Hank pulled her closer once they were standing next to his truck and gave her a hard, hot kiss that told her she wasn't the only one suffering and ready to ring the bell on round two.

"I want you to spend the night at my place again," he said as he released her.

She nodded. "Okay."

"Need to get anything from your apartment beforehand?"

Given her experience from the previous night, she knew she wouldn't need pajamas, she already had a toothbrush to use—he'd had a new one under the bathroom sink—and she liked the smell of his shampoo in her hair.

"No. I think I'm okay."

He waited a second before asking, "What do you do for birth control?"

Macie wasn't a blusher normally. It just wasn't something she'd ever suffered from. Probably because she was usually the most frank person in any conversation. Which was saying something, considering her dad had made embarrassing her an art form throughout her life.

But when she was with Hank, she could feel the flames licking her cheeks far too often.

"I think I'm going to make you a list of subjects that are too personal to—"

"Whiskey, the second I get you in my house, you're taking off those clothes and I'm taking you to my bed," he interjected. "What you use for birth control *is* my business."

"Thought the reason we couldn't have sex last night was because you were giving me time to think."

"You getting in this truck?"

She nodded, and only just barely restrained from adding a loud "hell yeah."

"Then you've had enough time to think."

Macie laughed. "Jesus, Hank. It hasn't even been twenty-four hours. Take it easy with the generosity."

He blew out a long breath. "It feels like a hell of a lot longer to me."

She wasn't sure how he did that, how he made her feel so special, so desirable, and damn if it wasn't working on her. Stealing pieces of her heart while making her so fucking horny, she thought she'd explode. Rather than admit that, she said, "I get the birth control shot. I'm up-to-date."

Hank helped her into the truck without another word. In fact, he didn't speak at all until he'd started the vehicle and pulled away from the curb. Even then, all he said was, "Good."

Fine, Macie decided. If this conversation didn't bother him, she sure as shit wasn't going to let it bother her. "So... you're not going to use a condom?"

He glanced over at her briefly. "I will if you want me to. Otherwise, I'm clean. Only been with one woman in the past twenty years, and the last time she and I had sex was two years ago."

She gave him a mischievous grin. "So what you're really saying is our first time isn't going to last long."

He chuckled. "No, angel. What I'm saying is if you want me to use a condom, you gotta say so now because we'll have to make a stop at the drugstore."

"Oh." Macie had never had sex with a guy who didn't

wear one. She started to say that, but what came out was, "Don't stop. It's fine."

He smiled. Then he winked at her. "And, Whiskey?"

"Yeah?"

"Don't worry about my staying power. Once I finally get inside you, I'm not going be in a hurry to leave again."

She twisted to face him as much as her seat belt would allow. "I'm going to hold you to that."

"So...Bruce and Frank?"

Macie laughed. "God. Don't remind me. Let's just say you're doing better than both of them. Never went on a second date with either."

"So neither one of them was the last lover, huh?"

She tilted her head and studied his face. "No."

Though he didn't take his eyes from the road, it was obvious he felt the heat of her stare when he asked, "Why are you looking at me like that?"

"Trying to decide if that question was based on curiosity or jealousy."

"Both," he admitted readily. "Don't tell me who. I don't want to know. Might have to kill the man."

Macie bit her lip and considered telling him anyway. In truth, it felt like something he should know. But part of her was worried. How would he react when he found out? Would it change things between them? This thing between them was so freaking new, she couldn't quite wrap her head around it.

"Maybe you should let me tell you," she said at last.

He narrowed his eyes; her tone had obviously told him he

might not like what she was going to say. "Wait 'til we get to my place."

"If I tell you now, you can turn around and head back to my apartment if you want."

"There's not a single name you could say that would change my mind about taking you to my bed."

She hoped that was true. "Okay." She decided to let it go until later. And then, because it was her, she picked up a new subject, telling Hank about the new kitten her cousin Jeannette had just adopted. Jeannette was in serious danger of becoming a cat lady.

Once Hank parked and turned the engine off, she reached for the door handle. Hank reached over and grasped her wrist gently. "Wait there."

He didn't give her a chance to ask why before he climbed out of the truck. When he walked around and opened her door for her, she understood.

"Very chivalrous," she teased when he helped her down.

"Not at all. Just the way a man should treat his lady. I'm always going to open doors for you."

"It's only our second date, Hank, and you're already talking marriage and calling me yours."

"We've been friends for a while now, Macie. It's not like we're strangers. I know you and you know me. Only thing that's changing is the kissing and where you're going to be spending most of your nights."

"Wow. I think you *do* know me."

"What do you mean?"

"You keep throwing all this twisted logic at my feet,

which speaks to my own warped view of the world and makes it really hard for me to argue with you."

He chuckled. "You want a fight?"

"Not really, but..." Again, she was a bit worried about the last-lover thing that was hovering over their heads.

Hank sighed. "Come on." He took her hand and led her to the house. "Sooner you speak your piece, the sooner I can get you naked."

She laughed despite her nervousness. Then she realized it wasn't just talking about the past that had her worried. It was crawling into bed with Hank. Her head had nearly blown off after each of those amazing orgasms last night, and that was with just his fingers and mouth.

There was something about the way he took control, in bed and out, that turned her on in ways she couldn't explain. Truth was she wasn't a fan of domineering men. But Hank seemed to be the exception to that rule.

Maybe it was because he wasn't demanding things she didn't want to give him. And maybe it was because she knew, deep down, if she said no, he would stop without question. She trusted him. Completely.

Once they entered the house, he closed the front door and turned to face her. "So out with it. Give me the name."

Macie took a deep breath and just said it. "Porter."

Hank's brows furrowed. "My ranch manager?"

She nodded.

"When?"

"It was shortly after Johnnie died." She had talked to Hank about her close friendship with Harley Mills' brother quite a lot over the past year. Hank had known who

Johnnie was. After all, Maris was a small town. But he admitted he hadn't really paid much attention at the time to Johnnie's death or the funeral. Mainly because Sharon had been dying around the same time. It was something they had in common, one of the things that had drawn them closer and helped forge their new friendship these last few months. They'd both suffered a painful loss recently.

"Didn't know you and Porter knew each other that well." His expression and his tone were wooden. Completely unreadable. Was he angry? Hurt?

"The truth is we didn't, really..." She paused. She probably wouldn't come out of this sounding too good.

"Just tell me what happened, Macie."

"I was in charge of closing up the restaurant one night. It was a weeknight and business had been slow. I was in no hurry to go home and cry myself to sleep over Johnnie, so I told my cousin Paige to take off early. Porter was the only one still there, drinking alone at the bar. I locked the door, poured myself a shot of bourbon and the two of us drank together. He was upset about..." She hesitated again.

"Sharon."

Macie nodded. "Sounded like he was close to her."

"He was," Hank confirmed.

"We both got tipsy. No," she amended. "We got drunk. One thing led to another and he walked me back to my apartment. Guess you can figure out the rest."

"Just that one time?"

"Yeah. We sort of needed somebody that night, but I swear, Hank, that's all it was. I mean, he's a nice guy and he was really sweet, but we were both in a bad place at the time. I haven't been pining for him or anything."

"I'm glad he was there for you."

Well, that sure as hell wasn't the response she'd expected. "What?"

"And I'm happy you were there for him. He needed you that night."

And there went another little bit of her heart. The man was laying claim to all of it. Hard and fast. "Hank?"

"Yeah, Whiskey?"

"Can we go to your bedroom now?"

Rather than respond with words, Hank cupped her cheeks and kissed her, his tongue sweeping inside her mouth. When he pulled away, he captured her gaze with his. "I want you, Macie Sparks. More than I've wanted anyone in a long time."

Grasping her hand, he led her to his bedroom. He closed the door and leaned against it. "Take off your clothes."

She shook her head. "I'm not taking off a stitch until you do. Last night, you kept on way too many clothes."

Hank unbuttoned his shirt and slipped it over his shoulders, dropping it to the floor.

Macie took a minute to admire the view. The previous evening, Hank had slipped to the bathroom after he'd untied her and returned in a T-shirt and lounge pants that he'd slept in all night.

Hank was older than her by just over a decade, but she liked the way he carried his years. As a rancher, he spent a lot of time outside, which meant his skin was naturally dark year-round. He wasn't a stranger to physical labor either. And rather than a smooth, bare chest, he had a fair amount of hair, mostly brown, but with just a few strands of gray.

"You okay, Macie?"

She nodded, her eyes remaining on his chest. She was going to enjoy petting him.

"You sure?"

His persistence had her looking up. "Yeah. Why?"

"You're not usually this quiet."

Macie grinned. "Just enjoying the view."

He gestured to her shirt. "How about giving me a chance to do the same?"

She'd been naked in front of him last night. His genuine appreciation of her body made it easy for her to tug off her own top. Then, without a moment's hesitation, she reached behind her back, unhooked her bra, and stripped it off as well.

Maybe if she distracted him with her tits, she could buy herself a little more time to admire him.

That plan failed. Hank was a doer, not an observer.

"Add the pants and panties to that pile while you're on a roll."

She unfastened her jeans. Slipping off her shoes, she slid everything down in one fell swoop and stepped out of it.

"Now you." She was no stranger to making her own demands.

Problem was, unlike her past lovers, Hank wasn't so easy to boss around. And he was never in a hurry. Which was only partly annoying because he sure as fuck knew how to pass the time.

He shook his head. "Not yet."

"Hank." She started to walk toward him, intent on helping him speed things along, but he lifted his hand.

"Stop right there."

Speaking of annoying things...

Hank gave her a command—a fucking command—in that tone of voice, and her body responded before her brain had a chance to give him the what-for.

"Get on the bed, Whiskey. Lay down on your back, open your legs and let me look at you."

Well, that seemed like a way to get things moving. She turned, taking in his room as she walked to his bed. It was a sturdy, four-poster king bed that matched the house. What gave her pause was the elegant red-silk bedding, the abundance of soft throw pillows, the rich beauty of it all.

It didn't fit Hank. It fit...

"Dammit," Hank muttered.

"It's okay," she said, aware her tone was too wooden for believability.

"I didn't think, Macie."

"Her sheets?"

"Sharon spent a lot of her last year in bed. She liked pretty things. Soft things."

"I see." She did. She saw it all. And she hated it.

Then she hated herself for feeling that petty, that stupid.

He stepped behind her, his hands resting on her waist loosely. While they both knew he could nudge her forward and put her wherever he wanted in that sexy-as-sin, domineering way of his, he simply held her. Gave her time to come to grips with something that hadn't bothered her until that moment.

"I'm sorry."

She nodded, feeling ridiculous for her sudden, uncontrollable jealousy of a dead woman and touched by the sincerity of his words. He had loved his wife. God, part of her undeniable attraction to him was the fact he had been a wholly devoted, loving husband.

Macie twisted to face him.

Hank gave her a gentle kiss on the cheek. "I should have changed the sheets."

"I'm being silly, I know that."

"No. You're not. Not at all. If you'll give me just a second..."

It was clear he was ready to strip the bed, get rid of all reminders of Sharon.

Macie held up her hand to stop him. "Don't. I'm okay now."

He studied her face closely, clearly checking for some sign she was lying.

"I'm serious." She was.

Hank nodded slowly. "Will it piss you off to know I sort of like that it bothered you?"

She narrowed her eyes. "You like that?"

He grinned and tightened his grip on her waist. "Means you're starting to care about me enough to be jealous. Now you know how I feel about Porter."

"You didn't act jealous when I told you. You said you were glad I was there for him."

"I *am* glad about that. But it's rare to feel just one way about something when it involves a person you care about. The understanding part of me spoke out loud, reassured you it was okay. Because it is. The jealous part of me kept quiet while plotting out all the ways I could make Porter pay for sleeping with you first."

She winced. "Poor Porter."

He winked, but didn't take back the threat.

She bit her lower lip and confessed the rest. "I'm starting to hate Sharon because she had you for twenty years, because you loved her so much. That's weird. And wrong, I know it."

"We're only human, Macie. Neither one of us is bad people for feeling the way we do."

She rose up on tiptoe to kiss him. Hank got her. After a lifetime of having most folks look at her like she was a lunatic, it was refreshing and exciting to have someone look inside her slightly twisted brain and make sense of it. More than that, he wasn't turned off by it.

"You going to get on that bed?"

He was still giving her the choice, but this time the clever man laced his tone with a dare. Which was like waving a red flag in front of a raging bull.

She stepped out of his arms and backed toward the bed. Once the back of her thighs hit the mattress, she sank down. Any issues she had with the silk comforter vanished the second her ass hit it. It really was soft. And sexy.

A girl could get used to this kind of indulgence. Beat the hell out of her cotton bed-in-a-bag set that she bought on sale at Walmart.

Hank remained where she left him, his gaze traveling down her body and back again.

"Like what you see?" she asked as she sat on the edge.

"I will. Once you do what I told you to."

She had hoped he would forget that last part. While Macie wasn't lacking in self-confidence, she wasn't experienced enough to feel comfortable putting it all out there for inspection.

"Hank—" she started.

He took the steps necessary to reach her, his strong hands gripping her ankles and tugging her legs apart. The element of surprise worked in his favor, because she was wide open with Hank kneeling between her legs before she even realized his intent.

"God, you move fast."

His eyes flashed to her face briefly before returning to her pussy. "Told you in the truck. My patience is running out."

That was all the explanation he offered as he leaned closer and ran his tongue along her opening.

Macie dropped to her back with a groan. "Holy shit."

Most guys acted like going down on a woman was a chore. Hank didn't seem to begrudge the task. He actually seemed to enjoy it.

With his fingers and tongue, he had her gasping for air and pleading for sex in no time at all. "Please, Hank."

She gripped his dark brown hair, loving the thickness of it, the way there was enough to tug. There were just a few strands of gray at the temples that she found completely adorable for some reason.

She intended to use her grip on his hair to her advantage, pulling it in hopes that he'd follow her direction. Macie wanted him on top of her, inside her.

He didn't move. She had to be hurting him.

"Stubborn man," she said, when he continued to play

with her—torment her—just enough to keep her on the edge without letting her go over. "Goddammit, Hank! I mean it. Either you fuck me now or..."

He lifted his head. "Or?"

She hadn't thought the threat through very well. Her initial intention had been to threaten to leave, but wild horses weren't dragging her out of this bed until she'd gotten what she wanted, so that seemed like a stupid thing to say.

"Or..." She couldn't come up with a single thing that would hurt him without taking her down as well. And she wasn't foolish enough to risk her own pleasure.

She lifted one shoulder and gave him a sheepish grin. "Please?" she tried, losing the haughtiness in her tone.

Hank rose, but didn't move to take off his jeans. Instead, he held her gaze, letting her squirm uncomfortably. She felt a bit like a naughty child about to be punished for stealing a cookie.

"I'm going to assume you trust me, Macie, because it would be damn reckless of you to go to bed with a man you didn't."

She didn't have a clue where he was going with that, so she simply agreed since it was true. "I trust you."

"I'm not one of those young bucks you're probably used to. The type of man who'll let you run roughshod over him just because he's smitten and wants in your pants."

Macie didn't bother to admit he'd done a fairly good job describing her past lovers. But that wasn't really the point of this conversation and she knew it. She sat up slowly, drawing her legs closed, despite the scowl it produced on his face. "What kind of man are you?"

"You want me to tell you? Or show you?"

Wow. That was a loaded question. Either he could warn her what she was in for, and then do it. Or he could just do it.

There was no denying whatever he said was going to happen. The only difference was she'd be forewarned. What she couldn't decide was if there was more danger in knowing what was coming or worrying about what was on the way?

What the hell? Macie loved a good surprise, and given Hank's talented way of making her forget her own name when he touched her, it wouldn't matter if she knew or not. She wouldn't have time to fret about it.

She spread her legs apart once more. "Do your worst." She was a pretty fair hand at dares herself.

Or so she'd thought.

Hank reached for her arm and turned her with ease. One second she was on her back, facing him. The next she was facedown on the mattress with Hank leaning over her, his chest on her back, pressing her down tightly.

"I'm not an easy lover, Macie." As he spoke, she felt his hands unbuckling his belt and pulling the leather from the loops. It slid slowly against the skin of her ass. He wanted her to feel it.

She recalled the way he'd tied her to his bed the previous night. If she hadn't been horny as hell and obsessed with changing his mind about fucking her, that might have clued her in to what he liked earlier.

"So..." She forced herself to say the words. "I'm guessing bondage would be included." Though she wasn't tied up at the minute, there was no escaping the overwhelming sense of being held captive. She was pinned to the bed and would remain there until he moved.

"Yes."

Then he placed the belt on the mattress next to her, eye level with where her head rested. "You want to hit me with that?"

"Yes."

She wasn't so innocent that his affirmation shocked her. Much. She recalled her night with Porter. He'd taken her from behind, and he'd spanked her ass a few times as he fucked her. It had made the whole experience hotter, more thrilling. It had hurt in a very good way, and she'd actually asked him to keep going after the first two spanks.

"That would hurt."

"Probably."

She turned to look at him over her shoulder. "What if I said no, said I didn't want that?"

His face, which had been way too intense, softened. "I'd put the belt away and you'd never see it again. But, Macie, I'm pretty sure you wouldn't hate it. In fact, I think you're going to like it."

"You know, I'm not completely green about all this stuff. I read books. Well, I mean, I read *one* book. And I watch porn online occasionally. Okay, I've watched *a lot* of porn. So I know what you're talking about. It's just, I've never really done any of that."

"There's a difference between never and never really."

"Porter spanked me a little bit when...we...um...I'm thinking now would be an excellent time to shut up."

"I see."

Yeah. She was afraid he did. And once again, she worried that her drunken one-night stand with Porter had the potential to ruin what she had no doubt was going to be the greatest relationship of her life before it even started.

"I'm sorry," she said.

"I'm not. I'm glad he exposed you to it."

"You are?"

"It's just a different way to have sex, Macie. And we won't do it all the time. A lot of nights, we're going to crawl into this bed and I'm going to make love to you, missionary style."

She considered that. "That sounds kind of boring now that you've offered up the kinky stuff."

He chuckled and kissed the back of her head. "Macie?"

"Yeah?"

"I'm done talking now."

She giggled until he stood up. Hank didn't complain when she rolled to her side to watch as he pushed down his jeans and boxers, toed off his shoes.

Hank definitely was *not* overcompensating for anything with his big truck.

"Big truck, big..." she murmured.

The edges of his mouth tipped up as he ran his hand from the root to the tip of his cock.

"Can I do that?" she asked.

He shook his head. "Later, Whiskey. Right now," he gestured with his hand for her to lie back down, "I want to be inside you."

She opened her legs in invitation and Hank stepped

between her knees, leaning over her as he guided his cock to her pussy.

He placed just the head inside before pausing. "You going to be okay with just missionary the first time, kinky girl?" he teased.

It was on the tip of her tongue to continue the joke, to make some comment like "if she had to," but Hank didn't give her the chance to reply.

He slammed in to the hilt with a thrust that pushed her a few inches across the bed. Her hands flew to his shoulders, then wrapped around his neck as she searched for some way to hold on. He took her Vin Diesel style, fast and furious.

"Lock your ankles around my waist," he demanded as he continued to piston inside her.

Macie had never been particularly vocal in bed, which was ironic considering she never shut up anywhere else. This time, remaining quiet wasn't an option. Hank produced a litany of groans, moans, grunts, curses, pleas and—Jesus—even an almost scream as she came so hard, her teeth rattled.

Her inner muscles clenched tightly as stars flashed, blinding her. Throughout her climax, Hank kept fucking her, taking her even harder, if that was possible.

"Can't. Take..."

He withdrew, flipping her to her stomach, plowing back inside. The change meant he was going deeper and stroking new hot spots. Hank reached around her waist with one hand, his fingers rubbing her clit in time with his pounding rhythm.

"Jesus Christ," she gasped, as a trickle of perspiration ran along her cheek. "Holy. Fuck."

She placed her hand on his wrist, intent on tugging his hand away from her clit. Not because she didn't love it, but because it felt almost too good. It was overwhelming, too much stimulation. Macie wasn't used to being out of control, and certainly not to this extreme.

"Move your hand."

She didn't, couldn't. She kept trying to pull his hand away even as he pounded inside her.

"Now, Macie."

She heard the words, knew he was serious, but she was in self-preservation mode. Fight or flight was starting to kick in. It was too fucking much.

Hank shrugged off her grip and then, mercifully, his hand left her clit.

At least, she'd thought it was mercy. Big mistake.

His palm struck her ass. Hard.

It stung and she screamed, tried to pull away. It was impossible.

Hank's cock was still buried deep, one hand gripping her shoulder, using that hold to drag her down on his upswings, adding to the pressure. With the other hand, he spanked her. When that hand got tired, he switched it up, using the right instead of the left to spank her other ass cheek.

Macie's orgasm struck like lightning, her back arching as her entire body shook.

Hank responded this time, his own climax following hers. He slowed his pace, slamming in just three more times as she milked him dry.

She felt the jets of come as they filled her, the sensation

novel, different, new. There was no condom there to catch the sticky stuff. Macie liked it.

She fell forward, completely lifeless until Hank slowly withdrew. His departure provoked a shudder and he claimed the spot next to her on the bed. Her head was turned away, but she didn't have the strength to lift it to face him. His hand rested on her sore ass.

Funny how she hadn't registered that pain until now. During the spanking, she'd only wanted more, each hard smack traveling straight to her pussy, making her insane with need.

Macie had no idea how long they lay there. She was pretty certain she'd dozed for a bit. When she finally found the strength, she lifted her head and turned to look at him.

Hank's eyes were open and he caught her gaze. "Okay?"

She nodded. "That was...really intense."

Macie had expected her words to provoke a smile, but this was Hank. Those grins were few and far between. Right now, he looked far too serious. And then she recalled Sharon. Remembered this was his first time with a woman since his wife had passed away.

"Are *you* okay?" she asked.

"Yeah." The word was right, but she didn't miss the slight hesitation before he spoke it.

She leaned up on her elbow, reaching out to run her hand over his chest. It felt odd to her that despite everything they'd just done, she hadn't had a chance to really touch him. Though it cost her to ask, she knew it would be better to find out now if he had regrets.

"Second thoughts?" she forced herself to ask.

He scowled. "Not a single one."

Those words came quickly, making it easier for her to breathe again. "I just thought maybe..." What was it about Hank that always had her scrambling to find her words? She didn't have this trouble with anyone else in the world. "I know you haven't been with anyone since Sharon, so—"

"Sharon?" He murmured the name so low she almost didn't hear it. "Shit."

Macie tilted her head. She didn't understand his response. "What?"

"I wasn't thinking about her, Macie. Not at all."

Ah. She got it. Here, she'd been thinking he was feeling guilty for, well, not necessarily cheating on his wife, but for not being faithful to her for the rest of his life. And now poor Hank was feeling bad because he hadn't thought of her at all.

"Sorry," she whispered. She was making a muck of this. Then she recalled his hesitation. "What were you thinking about then? That had you looking so serious?"

Hank sat up slowly, drawing her up as well. "I was afraid I'd hurt you."

She shook her head. "You didn't."

He raised his hand. "Wait. I didn't finish. I was afraid I'd hurt you, but I knew I couldn't apologize for it and I couldn't promise not to do it again. Because I want to do all of that to you again. That and even more. I'm not sure, I've never felt..."

She'd made Hank feel something new? It was like she'd won the lottery.

"Hank," she said, reaching for his hand. "I don't want you to say you're sorry. And I sure as hell don't want that damn promise."

He leaned forward and kissed her. It was a soft touch, sweet, romantic. Beautiful.

"Shower or sleep?" he asked when they parted.

"Does the shower come with you?"

Hank placed a playful kiss on the end of her nose as Macie struggled to keep up with him. He could shift from intense to sweet to silly in the blink of an eye. She loved it.

"Don't think you should plan on showering alone in this house very often."

"Come on." She shifted toward the end of the bed somewhat gingerly. Man, what a workout.

Hank noticed her discomfiture. "Change of plans. We're soaking in a hot bath together."

She sighed sleepily, not bothering to hide her grin or her outright infatuation with him. At this rate, there wouldn't be any pieces of her heart left that Hank hadn't claimed by morning.

CHAPTER FOUR

Hank climbed out of the truck and stretched. He'd just dropped Macie off at her apartment, so she could get ready for work. And he had every intention of being at the restaurant when she got off work. He wasn't willing to entertain the idea of not spending the night with her anytime in the near future, and he'd told her that in no uncertain terms.

She'd made some funny comment before they parted about how he really needed to brush up on his "playing it cool" skills. He'd given her a kiss that made sure she understood he never intended anything between them to be cool... or even lukewarm. She inspired heat, fire, flames, ravaging infernos.

Besides, he was too old to play all those stupid dating games. Hell, he hadn't done that when he was young. He'd laid eyes on Sharon when he was just twenty-two. They went out on all of six dates before he proposed. Porter had given him shit for rushing it, but even he had admitted several years after the wedding that Hank had found the perfect bride.

Crazy thing was...as certain as Hank had been about Sharon, he was even more sure of Macie. He was falling hard for the woman, and while it was becoming obvious that her experience when it came to romance and relationships was basically nonexistent, there was something about her that screamed forever. If the jackasses in Maris hadn't cottoned onto that long before now, that was their loss. Hank wasn't going to make the same mistake. They'd all had their chance and blown it. Now she was his.

The sound of a tool clinking against concrete and a muttered curse caught his attention. Porter was underneath their old ranch pickup, lying on a creeper, changing the oil. All Hank could see were the man's legs sticking out.

Hank stuffed the keys to his own truck in his front pocket and walked over. Time for a chat with his ranch manager.

Porter must have sensed his arrival because he requested a wrench as soon as Hank got within a few feet of him.

Hank retrieved the tool from the box nearby, then bent down to hand it Porter. He couldn't see the man's face. This conversation was one he wanted to have eye to eye. But he didn't get a chance to stall when Porter asked, "Where'd you take off to so early this morning?"

Macie had only been here two nights, and it was clear from his question Porter hadn't realized she'd been there.

"Had to take Macie back to town. She's working the lunch and dinner shifts."

Porter's body went still. "Macie, huh?"

As far as replies went, that one was damn vague. "She's spent the last couple of nights here."

Whatever shock he might have experienced appeared to

have passed as Porter started working again. Neither of them said anything else as Porter removed the plug and Hank listened as oil began draining out. Porter wheeled himself out on the flat cart and then sat up.

His gaze met Hank's. "'Bout time you made your move."

Hank nodded. "Not that easy to just hop back in the saddle, Port."

"Yeah, I get that, man." Porter Cormack was more than Hank's ranch manager, he was his best friend. The man had come to work on the Cooper ranch back when Hank's daddy ran the place. They'd worked side by side then as hands. They'd break their backs during the week on the ranch, and then tear it up on the weekends, doing more than their fair share of drinking and partying. All of that felt like a lifetime ago.

Hank's father had a stroke well over two decades earlier and died within weeks. Hank's partying years were cut short. It had been up to him to take over the family business, so he'd proposed to Sharon, the girl he was sweet on shortly after his father's funeral, married her, moved her in with him and his mother, and promoted Porter to ranch manager.

Porter, a good friend, had eschewed the bar scene with him, declaring it was time they both grew up and got their shit together. However, unlike Hank, Porter hadn't met a woman able to drag him to the altar. A confirmed bachelor, Porter claimed he was happy with his life just like it was.

Hank's mother only lived a few years longer than his father. With his daddy gone, it was as if she'd lost the will to live. At that point, Porter and Sharon became Hank's family. And when Sharon passed, that family shrunk to just the two of them. Which was why this conversation needed to happen.

"She told me about the two of you and the night you spent together."

Hank had to hand it to Porter. The man had one hell of a poker face, always playing his cards close to his chest.

"Okay." Porter's voice was deep, quiet, emotionless.

"Sort of surprised you never mentioned it."

"She told you when it happened?"

Last year. Right after Sharon's death. "She did. And I can see keeping it quiet at the time, but..." But it had become increasingly obvious in the last few months that Hank was interested in Macie. Hell, Porter was the one to point that out.

"You and Macie are a good match. Didn't want to get in the way of you asking her out. Figured what happened between her and me didn't matter. It was one time. Neither of us was looking for more than that night. And to be honest, there was a lot of whiskey involved."

"Yeah. That's what she said."

"She was torn up about her friend Johnnie's death, and..."

Porter didn't bother to finish his thought, but Hank got it just the same. Neither one of them was very good at saying Sharon's name out loud to each other. Even now. Her death had left a hole. In both of their lives.

"You sure you're okay with me and Macie being together?" Hank forced himself to ask.

Porter gave him a curious look. "Why wouldn't I be? Hell, man, I was the one who told you to pull your thumb out and ask the girl for a dance."

Hank shrugged. "Maybe so, but, well...dammit, you were there first."

Porter laughed. "So what?"

"So I feel like I might have stepped on your toes or something. I mean, Macie's a hell of a catch."

Porter rolled his eyes. "Jesus, Coop. You've got it bad. Macie is a handful on a good day and most men in town know that. You're the only one who doesn't seem to get worn out by all that talking of hers. So believe me when I say, I'm fine letting you take that whirlwind on."

Hank frowned, unable to understand how Porter could have had Macie in his arms for a single second and let her go. "You're kidding, right? Macie is as sweet as they come."

For a moment, it appeared Hank had rendered his friend speechless.

When Porter failed to respond, Hank continued, "There's not a damn thing hard about being with her. She's beautiful, straightforward, honest. I never have to guess what she's thinking."

Porter's grin grew as Hank made his list. "Yeah. That. Right there. The woman tells you every thought in her head. As she's having them."

Hank lifted one shoulder casually, dismissing that complaint. "I don't mind. I think she's interesting. Funny."

"Which is why the right man is dating her. It's cool, Coop. You didn't steal my thunder or my girl or whatever it is you're worrying about. You and Macie are a good couple and," Porter paused, swallowing heavily, "I'm really glad you found her. Unlike me, you were not made to live alone. You were born to love a woman. She's lucky to have you."

And then, because it appeared to have embarrassed him to have said something nice, Porter turned away from him, opening up a fresh can of oil. "Not sure oil is going to make this hunk of junk run any better."

Before Hank could thank him for the kind words, the sound of a car coming down their lane caught his attention.

Porter's murmured "shit" clued him in to who was arriving even before he turned around. Hank had been surprised Janice hadn't made an appearance at his place last night, questioning him about Macie, but then he remembered Wednesday was her book club night. Sharon had been in the same club, attending the meetings right up until the cancer left her too weak to walk.

He forced himself not to scowl as Janice parked the car and emerged. She smiled and waved, but Hank didn't return either gesture. In truth, his patience with his wife's best friend was at an end.

Sharon, God bless her, had asked Janice to keep an eye on him after her passing. Somewhere along the line, Janice had changed the interpretation of that request from something friendly to something much more. In her mind, she'd twisted those words to mean she should be the next Mrs. Hank Cooper, and while he had taken care thus far not to hurt her feelings—out of respect for Sharon—that kindness was wearing thin.

"Janice," he said.

"Hey, Coop, Porter," she said with a sunny smile. She was a friendly, if flighty, woman. He'd teased Sharon a bit when she was alive, constantly wondering how an intelligent woman such as her could hang around with an airhead like Janice.

"Janice," Porter said, looking far too pleased when he plopped himself back down on the low cart and wheeled himself under the truck once more. Bastard had found an escape. Porter had been telling Hank for weeks he was going to have to be more forceful with Janice. Simply telling the woman he wasn't interested in dating her clearly wasn't enough.

Thing was, Hank's daddy had raised him to be respectful of women, and he was afraid nothing short of hurting Janice's feelings was going to convince her to move on.

Janice held out a loaf of homemade applesauce cake. "I was baking this morning and thought I'd bring you by a treat. I know how you love my applesauce cake."

Hank took the loaf and thanked her. One of the main reasons he'd started taking so many meals at Sparks Barbeque was to avoid Janice, who'd stopped by almost nightly with a plate of food for him right after Sharon's death.

"I was wondering if you wanted to come over for dinner tonight. I'm making your favorite," she added, "fried chicken."

Hank took a deep breath. Time to let her down. Again. "I can't, Janice. I've got plans with Macie."

Janice tilted her head. "What sort of plans?"

"A date."

"Another one?"

He nodded. "I'm going out with Macie now."

Janice laughed as if he'd told a funny joke. Hank wasn't

sure how to react to that. Half the time, he didn't have a clue what Janice was thinking.

"She's a bit young for you, isn't she? Is this some sort of midlife crisis thing?"

He shook his head, fighting hard to hold on to his temper. "Not at all. She's my girlfriend."

Janice didn't appear to pick up on his tone. A wise person would have known he was annoyed, and backed off.

"Well, I'm sure she's the perfect person for you to dip your toes back into the water with. After all, she's a professional dater, isn't she? Figure you're about the only man in Maris she hasn't gone out with."

Hank heard a soft groan from beneath the truck behind him. Porter was listening to every word, and even *he* knew she's just crossed a very big line.

"I don't think that's true at all. And I'm not dipping my toe in anything, Janice. Macie and I are dating. And it's serious." At least, it was in his mind.

He was worried he might still have to convince Macie his feelings were sincere. For as confident as the woman was, Macie had mentioned not being his type a couple of times since their first date. Apparently, she felt the shadow of Sharon hovering over her. He supposed that was to be expected. He had been married for a long time. Obviously it was going to take him more than just three days to convince Macie *she* was his type too.

Janice smiled, almost indulgently. "I understand."

Hank was fairly certain she didn't. But this time he was determined to put an end to whatever foolish nonsense she'd cooked up in her head that had her thinking he was ever going to ask her out. "You do? You understand that she's my girlfriend and that, much as I appreciate the meals and the baked goods and stuff, it's really not appropriate for you to keep stopping by like this?"

Janice nodded and pointed at the loaf of applesauce cake. "Of course I do. Enjoy that." With that, she walked back to her car. "I'll see you again soon," she called out as she got in and drove away.

Porter slid back out from under the truck.

"Thanks for the support there, buddy," Hank said, sarcastically.

Porter gave him a shit-eating grin. "Oh, sorry. Didn't realize you needed help."

"Jackass."

"You're going to have to be more direct than that, Coop."

Hank suspected his friend was right, but the contrary part of him spoke up instead. "What's more direct than telling her Macie is my girlfriend and to stop coming by?"

Porter shook his head. "Not sure, but there's no way she would have acted as breezy and carefree as she just did if she'd really given up on you. That woman's tenacious as a bulldog with a bone."

"Last six times she's been here, I've told her I don't want to date her. Ever. I'm not sure what the hell else I'm supposed to do. Tattoo it on my forehead?"

"Not sure even that would be enough. Woman is fixated on you and this future she's created in her head—with your dead wife's permission."

Hank sighed. "I know. Sharon would know how to deal

with this, but..." He shrugged, unable to speak the rest of his thought.

"But if Sharon was here, you wouldn't have this trouble," Porter finished.

"To hell with Janice. I've told her I'm dating Macie. Maybe once she's seen the two of us together a few times, it'll sink in and she'll move on."

Porter didn't look convinced. "Maybe."

"You finished changing that oil?"

Porter shook his head. "Nope. Was too busy hiding under the truck. I'll wrap it up now."

Hank chuckled. "Coward. I'm gonna get some stuff done in the barn."

Hank spent the better part of the next two hours working on repairing a broken chainsaw. He'd just finished when he heard another car coming down the lane.

Jesus Christ. He wiped his hands off and stormed out of the barn, ready to tell Janice—once and for all—to stay the fuck away from him. He was done being nice.

He rounded the corner just as Macie closed her car door and started toward him. She stopped suddenly, frowning when she saw his face.

"Um, sorry," she muttered. "This is obviously a bad time."

Hank lifted one hand quickly and shook his head. One look at her and the fury he felt vanished. "No, no. It's a good time."

"You just looked really pissed off to see me."

Hank walked toward her. "I'm never going to be pissed off to see you, Whiskey." He grasped her waist and pulled her close, stealing a quick kiss. "Didn't expect to see you back here so soon. Did you forget something?"

She tightened her grip around his neck and stole a kiss of her own, adding some tongue and letting it linger just long enough to send all the blood in his body straight to his dick.

"No. I brought lunch for you. I didn't cook it," she was quick to reassure him as she pointed toward the plastic bag she'd placed on the hood of her car. "It's from the restaurant. Sort of planned to use that as an excuse to come see you. Was going to surprise you with a picnic. But the truth is, I missed you. And I'm horny as shit."

Hank laughed. "You don't need to use food as an excuse to visit, Macie. Hell, just the horny part would be enough reason for me."

"I was taking you at your word when you said I didn't have to play things cool. So I hope it's not freaking you out that I'm back here already. Does this make me look clingy or needy?"

He kissed her gently on the cheek. She was a breath of fresh air. Her honesty, her willingness to put herself out there so completely, was probably one of the things he found most attractive about her. "Nope. Truth is, I was just finishing up my chores and fighting like the devil not to get into my truck and drive to you."

She ran her hand down the front of his chest, her fingers toying with the buttons on his shirt. "I wouldn't have complained."

"This way is better. Means the difference between me taking you on a flat surface in the privacy of my house or up against a wall in the storage closet of the restaurant with half your family outside the door."

Macie snorted. "God. What does it say about me that I think both those options sound hot as hell?"

"It says you're perfect for me." Hank backed her toward the side of the barn, pressing closer to give her a much deeper kiss. Macie gave herself up to it—and him—without reservation. Her hands slid around his waist, tugging his shirt out of his jeans so she could slip her fingers beneath to stroke his bare back.

Hank's fingers did some exploring themselves, finding her breasts and cupping them, before squeezing more firmly. Macie groaned against his lips, the sound fueling his need even more.

"Jesus. Don't make me turn the hose on you two."

Hank slowly withdrew from the embrace at the sound of Porter's voice.

Macie glanced over toward his ranch manager. "Hey, Porter."

"Hey, Mace." Porter was grinning at the two of them. "That's quite a show you're putting on there, but you might want to have mercy on the dozen or so single guys around here who still have a day's worth of work to do. Making it pretty hard for us to concentrate."

"Good point. Time to move this inside." Hank grasped Macie's hand and started to lead her to the house. He was surprised when she resisted.

"What about the food?"

"Food?" Porter asked.

Macie laughed and pointed toward her car when it

became apparent Hank wasn't turning around for a couple of sandwiches. "It's in the bag. Help yourself," she called over her shoulder.

Once they entered the house, Hank closed the door, then turned and pressed Macie against it, resuming the kiss they'd started by the barn.

"I missed you too," he murmured as he pulled her T-shirt over her head. "I thought you had to work. How much time do we have?"

"Got my dad to man the bar for me. Jackass never does any work these days. It'll be good for him." As she spoke, Macie kicked off her shoes.

"He didn't mind?" he asked as he unfastened her jeans and worked the denim over her hips and off.

"Nope. He's over the moon about you and me. The man's way too obsessed with me getting married and giving him grandbabies."

Macie, whose hands had been roaming all over his chest, froze. "I mean, not that I think...that we're..." She blew out a frustrated breath. "That came out wrong. I know we've only been seeing each other a few days. I wasn't implying that..." Once again, she stopped, clearly struggling to dig herself out of what she presumed was one hell of a hole.

Hank let her off the hook—as he unhooked her bra. "Whiskey, you're talking to a man who was happily married for twenty years. The idea of weddings and kids doesn't freak me out in the slightest. I liked being married a hell of a lot better than being alone."

"Yeah, but, God, I swear sometimes it's like my mouth is moving twenty miles ahead of my brain."

"Just part of your charm."

"No one else has ever found that charming."

"The world is full of idiots."

Their conversation ended when Hank bent his head and sucked one of her nipples into his mouth. Macie's hands flew to his head as her own flew back against the door.

"Oh my God. This. This is what I missed. I don't know what you've done to me, Hank Cooper, but I'm so fucking addicted to this. To you."

"Good," he murmured, as he continued to suckle on her nipple, dragging one finger along the slit between her thighs.

Macie was wet and squirming for more.

"We're not going to make it to the bedroom," he said as he lifted his head. Wrapping one arm around her waist, he propelled her toward the living room. Pressing her back on the couch, he unhooked his own jeans, pushed them just below his hips, tugged out his cock, knelt between her outspread legs and thrust into heaven.

Finesse was not the order of the day. He took Macie hard and fast, rutting like a dog in heat as her back arched and her eyes closed. Rubbing her clit, he drove her to orgasm fast, loving the way her pussy clenched against his hard flesh. Hank continued to thrust throughout—feeling the peak of her climax and then the slow ebbing.

Once she landed, he increased his pace, driving her back up. When she came a second time, he was there with her, emptying himself into her, loving her hoarse cries and the way her body trembled as her orgasm waned.

He held himself over her with his elbows on the couch. It

took them several minutes to catch their breath enough to speak.

"Would you laugh if I broke into the chorus of 'Afternoon Delight'?" Macie asked.

"Jesus. That's an old one."

"My mom loves that song. Which is now a very disturbing fact, so maybe we'll just skip the song after all."

Hank winked. "Much as I love the idea of you serenading me, I need to get back to work."

Macie sighed. "Yeah. Me too. Dammit."

Hank rose slowly, hitching his jeans back around his hips and fastening them. Meanwhile, as always, Macie's clothes were too far away to reach. "How come I'm always naked and you're barely undressed?"

"Thought we covered that already."

"Lord-of-the-manor thing still in effect?"

"Always." Hank tugged her onto his lap, cuddling her. He was thrilled she'd shown up here on her own to surprise him. "How late do you work tonight?"

She grimaced. "I'm closing. Won't get off until after eleven. Probably too late for me to drive out here."

He agreed. He didn't want her on the road alone that late. "So I'll meet you at your place after."

"Really?" Her face reflected pure delight.

"Give me your key. I'll meet you in your bed at eleven-fifteen."

"Naked," she said resolutely. "I want you to be naked. My place, my turn to be lady of the manor."

Hank chuckled. "I look forward to watching you try."

"I'm sure you do." Her tone and expression told him she

already knew it was a lost cause. He'd never handed the reins over in the bedroom and he didn't intend to start now. Old dog. New tricks. Not happening. But knowing his girl, she was still going to give it a run for her money.

"Your family going to give you a hard time when you go back to work?"

Macie shrugged. "They'll probably tease me a little bit. My dad will caution me not to scare you away like all the other fellas in town. But other than that...well...let's face it, what you and I have going on here is vanilla city compared to Jeannette and her firefighters, and Tyson's new relationship with Harley and Caleb."

"I've never been called vanilla before."

She laughed. "Aw. Did I hurt your big studly male pride?"

He tickled her as she fought to escape, trying to squirm away. Hank guided her to her back on the couch once more, covering her. "Don't poke the bear."

She drove one finger into his waist a few times. "Poke. Poke."

Hank recalled Macie's concern over her one-night stand with Porter and her need to be completely honest with him. He owed her the same. He remained above her, caging her beneath him. His actions weren't as subconscious as they should be. In truth, he was making sure she couldn't run if she didn't like what he told her next.

"You ever consider a threesome?" he asked.

Macie snorted. "In case you failed to notice, Hank, I've spent this long finding just *one* guy who could tolerate me with my constant chatter, off-color humor and never-ending opinions. By the way, I'm not sure what that says about you. You might want to consider talking to a therapist."

He chuckled at her joke. "I'm being serious. Pretend it's in the realm of possibility. Would you want to do that?"

"Are you worried this is a family trait?"

"Do I sound worried?"

Something sparked in her eyes and he watched as she processed his question. "Have you ever?" She paused and reconsidered. "But no. You couldn't. You and Sharon. Never mind."

"I've done the threesome thing, Macie."

Her eyes went wide. "Seriously? When? With who? How the hell did you manage to keep that a secret in this town?"

"With Sharon. And Porter."

Her eyebrows furrowed as she tried to piece together what he was telling her. Before she could get too carried away, he quickly explained, not wanting her to jump to the wrong conclusions.

"Sharon wanted to try it. So Porter and I surprised her on her birthday. Don't get me wrong, Mace. Sharon and me, we were a couple. Just the two of us. But Porter, well, every now and then, he'd join us in bed."

"So it was more sex position than relationship?"

He shrugged. "I guess that's one way to say it."

"Did you and Porter—"

Hank shook his head. "We were there for Sharon. Not each other."

If he expected to render Macie speechless, he was a fool. Nothing seemed to knock her down.

"And you're saying that you would," she bit her lower lip for just a moment, "want to do that with me?"

"Whiskey, we'll never do anything you don't want to do, that you're not comfortable with."

"Did you and Porter talk about this?"

"No. Absolutely not. I don't want secrets between us, Macie. There's nothing that's happened in your past that will change the way I feel about you today. You understand that, right?"

She nodded and he could see she was finally starting to believe him about that.

He decided to drive home another point while he was at it. "I don't want you to be afraid to ask me for anything you might want."

"Like Sharon asked you for the threesome?"

"Like that."

As always, her thoughts went off in a completely different direction. "Do you think we're going too fast?"

He grinned. "I don't. But if you do, we can slow down."

Macie dismissed that offer in an instant. "Oh no. I don't want that. I've waited a lifetime for something like this. It's romantic. And hot. And I like it. A lot. I like *you* a lot."

Hank kissed the end of her nose. "I like you too, Whiskey. A lot."

CHAPTER FIVE

MACIE OPENED HER EYES, blinking against the sunlight that shone through the window. The first thing her gaze landed on was the rose lying on the pillow next to her.

Hank wasn't in the bed, so he'd left a flower in his place. She was tempted to pinch herself to make sure this was all still real.

The two of them had slept together every single night for three weeks. Most of the time they stayed at the ranch, but on nights when she worked late, Hank would wait for her at her apartment. And while he granted her wish that he always be naked in her bed, that was pretty much the only command he took.

Instead, he was usually the one making sensual, kinky, gorgeous demands. Somehow, the man had persuaded her into doing a striptease for him, while wearing his cowboy hat and dancing to Joe Cocker's "You Can Leave Your Hat On." He'd tied her spread eagle to his bed countless times—the man was a huge fan of bondage. He'd tossed her over his lap twice and spanked her into orgasm. He'd taken her in the storage closet at the restaurant, but mercifully, he'd waited until the place was closed and everyone gone, though he'd promised that wouldn't always be the case. They'd taken countless showers and baths together. They'd christened the hayloft in his barn, her kitchen floor, the back of his truck, and made love on a blanket under the stars. They'd gone skinny-dipping at the lake, and last night, he'd taken her missionary style—something that was seven hundred miles from boring with Hank—in his candlelit bedroom on a bed of rose petals.

She was so in love it was ridiculous.

And that feeling doubled instantly when she caught the scent of bacon frying in the air.

Macie rose, glancing around the room. She grinned when she realized her clothes were nowhere to be found. Hank loved to hide them from her, insisting that it was fine for her to walk around naked.

Now, as always, she rifled through his dresser, tugging out one of his large T-shirts and pulling it on. The man was persistent.

She padded downstairs barefoot. She had the day off and she was hoping to entice him into playing hooky as well.

Pausing at the entrance to the kitchen, she leaned against the doorjamb and watched as he cooked up a breakfast fit for a king. He wore faded, loose-fitting jeans and a T-shirt, his typical work attire. The tray on the counter next to him told her he'd intended to bring the food to her in bed.

For a second, she considered sneaking back upstairs. She'd never had a man bring her breakfast in bed. But Hank turned around and caught her watching him before she could escape.

His gaze narrowed when he spotted her in his T-shirt. Glancing over, she saw her clothing, folded neatly on a chair in the corner.

"Stealing my shirts again?"

She pointed to her clothes. "Tit for tat, hotshot."

His eyes fell to her breasts and she rolled her eyes.

"So I say the word 'tit' and you feel compelled to ogle mine?" she teased.

"You're the one walking around without a bra. Lift that damn shirt up. Give me a morning treat."

"It's been weeks, Hank. You would think you'd be a bit bored of that view by now."

"Never gonna happen." He waved the spatula, indicating his request still stood.

She lifted the shirt, giving him a quick peek-a-boo of not just her breasts, but also the fact she hadn't bothered with panties, before pulling it back down again.

Hank turned to the stove and pulled the pan off the heat.

Before she could figure out what he was doing, he was across the room. He took the front hem of the shirt and tugged it over her head, exposing her entire front, while leaving the shirt on her arms and back.

"What about my breakfast?" she asked, even though food was the absolute last thing she wanted at the moment. Which was somewhat shocking to her because...well...bacon.

Hank cupped her breasts, almost aggressively, squeezing them roughly in his large, calloused hands. God, she loved it when he went all caveman alpha male on her.

She pressed her legs together when her pussy fluttered in response.

"Thanks for the flower," she whispered, when he kissed her cheek.

"Thank you for last night."

The man was diabolical. By mentioning the previous night, he'd taken her arousal up at least three more notches. Because last night had been amazing.

"Go bend over the table, Whiskey. Facedown. I'm going to fuck that pretty pussy of yours from behind."

"You sweet talker." He kissed her, fast and hard, before she moved across the room to do exactly what he asked.

Macie had never, not once, managed to resist one of his deep-voiced commands. Maybe one day, she'd find the willpower to play with him a bit, see what he'd do if she disobeyed. Something told her it would be worth it for the punishment, but she was never able to resist taking him up on his offers.

She tossed the shirt off completely before bending over the way he requested. When he remained where he was, she lifted up on her tiptoes and wiggled her ass at him.

He chuckled at her impatience, but gave in to her unspoken request that he get the lead out.

Stepping behind her, he ran his hands over her bare ass. Part of her expected him to spank her, but instead, he kept his touches gentle, soft caresses.

"Spread your legs apart."

She did so, shivering slightly when the cool air hit her pussy. She was so hot, so ready.

Hank ran his finger along her slit, from clit to anus. Last

night, he'd coated two fingers with lube and fucked her ass with them. It had been their first foray into anal play, but there was no question it wouldn't be the last. She'd loved it. And given her very vocal climax, Hank knew it.

Macie released a sigh when she heard Hank tug down the zipper on his jeans. While she was a big fan of his foreplay, she was equally enamored of the times when he just got right down to business.

Hank leaned over her, placing a quick kiss on her bare shoulder. "Don't want to play, huh?"

She'd clearly given away her relief. "I'm thinking sex, bacon and then cuddling. We can do double foreplay tonight."

"Good plan," he replied with a chuckle. His cock nudged against her opening as he slid in slowly.

Once he was seated to the hilt, she expected him to keep going. She was surprised when he stopped.

Glancing over her shoulder, she realized he wasn't looking at her. Instead, his gaze was focused on something in the kitchen.

She followed that look, surprised when she discovered Porter standing at the back door. From the expression on his face, it was clear he hadn't intended to interrupt.

She expected Porter to offer a quick apology and back out, so she was shocked when Hank chose that moment to start moving.

Macie's gaze was still focused on Porter's face. He glanced from her, to Hank, then back again.

"Do you want him to leave, Macie?" Hank asked as he continued to rock inside her.

Her mind whirled over the question and what it meant. Hank had told her about his threesome with Porter and Sharon weeks ago. Since then, he'd never mentioned it again.

"I..." She didn't have a clue what to say.

"There's no right or wrong answer, Whiskey," Hank assured her, even as he kept fucking her...in front of Porter, who'd gone still as a statue. "Just tell me what you want. What you *really* want."

Porter's eyes met hers and she saw the same desire she'd seen that night a year ago. While they weren't compatible in terms of a love match, there had been no denying their bodies liked each other just fine.

Rather than respond, Macie lifted her chest up from the table, giving Porter a much better view of her breasts. They swayed as Hank began to thrust inside harder, faster.

"Macie." Porter whispered her name, the sound so quiet in the room, she read her name on his lips rather than hearing it.

She forced herself to keep her eyes open, locked with Porter's. Hank reached around her sides and took her breasts in his hands, cupping them, using them for purchase as he fucked her even harder.

Macie couldn't hold back her groans or the orgasm that was moving in faster than a hurricane in September.

"God, Hank," she gasped.

Her words prompted more strength from her lover. The table squeaked against the tile floor, moving an inch or so with each inward thrust.

Porter walked across the room, placing his thighs against the table, holding it still, making Hank's motions more potent, more powerful. Macie held her chest up with her elbows on the surface. Porter was tall, like Hank, so it was hard to keep her eyes on his face. She studied his chest instead as Hank took her.

Until Hank's fingers gripped her hair tightly, tugging her face upward, forcing her to see the impact their fucking was having on Porter.

God, he wanted her too.

"Do you like this, Macie?"

She couldn't speak, her breath coming too harshly, too loudly. Her heart was racing, with sheer excitement, arousal, and maybe even a little bit of fear. It was a potent combination.

She was naked between two fully dressed men, being fucked by one as the other watched. Single hottest moment of her life.

"Don't stop talking now, Mace. Tell me." Hank's voice was deep, demanding.

"I love it. So fucking much."

Her words seemed to free whatever grip Porter had on his emotions. She saw relief in his eyes. And so much need it almost hurt her to look at him.

Hank released his grip on her hair as his hands moved to her waist. He was close to the end. She could feel it.

Her gaze drifted lower as she spied the hard-on Porter was packing behind his jeans. She considered reaching out, but she was stopped when Porter shook his head.

He still leaned against the table, pushing against it to hold it steady for Hank's thrusts.

"Not this time," Porter murmured.

His comment obviously captured Hank's attention, clued her lover in to her intentions.

Hank reached for her wrists and tugged them behind her back, holding them tightly with one hand. The restraint forced her chest back to the table's surface.

Macie closed her eyes then, gave herself up to the moment, let go of every single thought racing through her mind and just let herself feel.

Her body trembled as her orgasm began. Hank kept her hands secured with one of his, his other hand gripped her hip. She was vaguely aware of another hand, stroking her hair gently.

Macie came loudly and Hank was with her, filling her with come as his climax shook the table. For several seconds afterward, Macie lay still, her cheek pressed against the table, her eyes closed.

Part of her was afraid to open them, to face what they'd just done.

Hank must have recognized her hesitance. He placed a soft kiss on her cheek. "It's okay, Macie."

"I can't believe we...I didn't know..." Her eyes flew open. She narrowed them as she looked over her shoulder at Hank, frustration taking over. "Why can't I ever express a complete thought with you? I don't have this trouble with anyone else."

"Did you like that?"

Leave it to Hank to cut to the chase. "Yeah. I did. This doesn't make me like a slut or anything, does it?"

Hank chuckled while Porter groaned. "I'm going to let you field that one, bro."

Macie looked up just in time to see Porter walking toward the back door. Without another word, he was gone.

"What did I say?"

"You spoke your mind. Porter's intimidated by that. He's never really mastered the art of talking to women."

"Just fucking them, huh?"

"I'm sure he wouldn't appreciate that description, but yeah, maybe. He's more the strong, silent type."

"Funny. That's sort of how I think of you."

Hank helped her rise from the table, tugging her into his embrace. "Not always easy to get a word in edgewise with you, Whiskey. Be surprised if most men didn't come across that way to you," he joked.

She lifted her head so that he could see her face and feigned annoyance. "You asked me what I thought."

"I did."

Macie reached for the T-shirt she'd tossed to the floor earlier and pulled it back on. "Well, that was something," she said. Her wits were slowly beginning to return. And with them, her voice. "Certainly didn't expect that when I got out of bed this morning."

Hank grinned. "Me either."

"You're really okay with it?"

Hank hesitated just a heartbeat too long. "Yes."

He was lying. She could tell. And it pissed her off. So she gave him another shot at the truth.

"Really?"

He nodded, his response quicker this time. "I told you, Macie, there's nothing I won't give you. I love you."

It was the first time he'd ever said those words. Though

Macie had felt his love, almost from the very beginning, hearing him admit it filled her with so much emotion, it seeped out before she could stop it.

Tears sprang to her eyes.

"Dammit," she whispered. She was not a sappy person, not a crier. Unless she saw one of those Facebook clips people always shared of military men coming home to their delighted dogs, who would leap into their arms and make those pitiful, beautiful wailing sounds. Those videos always prompted a big cry, but other than that, she was solid as a rock.

Hank spotted the tears instantly, cupping her cheeks. He pressed his forehead against hers and closed his eyes. "I never thought I'd feel this way again. When Sharon died, I thought she'd taken my heart with her. You've proven me wrong."

And with that, she was completely undone. She sniffled loudly as a sob escaped.

"Dammit," she repeated. "I hate crying. Makes me look awful."

He grinned. "You're beautiful. You're always beautiful."

Her throat had seized up on the tears that were now pouring out of her eyes, but that didn't stop her from choking out the words she'd waited an entire lifetime to say. "I love you too." In her mind, she'd always imagined herself sounding much sweeter as she'd speak them softly to the man who stole her heart.

Instead they came out too loud and hoarse and hiccupy.

Hank didn't appear to mind that he'd just opened his heart up to a blubbering fool. He hugged her tightly once more, gracing her with the single biggest smile she had ever seen on his face.

He didn't say any more. He just held on to her until she pulled herself together. Then he blotted her face with a napkin, fried her up some more bacon, tugged her onto his lap and fed her.

Sex with Hank, and bacon.

Sort of made her want to pray for immortality.

Because there was no way Heaven could top this.

CHAPTER SIX

HANK AND MACIE swayed in the front porch swing, enjoying the beautiful evening and the soft breeze blowing. Less than a week had passed since Hank had confessed his feelings to her. Since that first date, the two of them had been inseparable. Macie had stopped offering to work double shifts at the restaurant. And if it weren't for Porter and his ranch hands picking up the slack, Hank might have lost the ranch.

He had been the poster child for responsible since his father's death, but any semblance of him being an adult had fallen to the wayside in the last seven days. He was worse than an alcoholic, so drunk on the love he felt for Macie, it consumed his every waking minute. And more than a fair share of his dreams each night.

The worst part was he couldn't shake himself out of the bliss enough to give a damn. He hadn't been this happy in years—Jesus, maybe ever—and he was going to enjoy it.

"You realize it's our anniversary. One month to the day

since you dragged me and my hairy legs out of the restaurant and fed me spaghetti."

"Damn. Wish you'd mentioned that earlier. I would have taken you and your hairy legs out to dinner to celebrate."

Macie snuggled closer to him, wrapping her arm around his waist and resting her head on his shoulder. "I think you should know that this is officially my longest relationship ever."

Every time Macie talked about her complete lack of long-term relationships, Hank was floored. At thirty-one, he figured a woman as beautiful and fun as her should have had at least a dozen former boyfriends. Hell, he couldn't believe she wasn't married with a couple kids already. Maris might be a small town, but it wasn't that damn small and there was no shortage of available men.

"Still find that hard to believe."

She lifted her head and gave him a quick kiss on the cheek, taking his amazement as a compliment, the way she always did. But that never answered his burning curiosity about why she'd never dated seriously.

"You gonna tell me why this is the longest relationship?"

Macie grinned and gave him that look that told him she was going to make a joke of it all. He shook his head, his expression stern. He really wanted to know the real reason.

"It's a serious question, Mace. Answer it."

"Or..." she baited. "What? You'll spank me?"

He rolled his eyes. The woman liked that too much, which meant spankings would never be something he could use as a punishment. "Or I'll put you in bed and sleep on the couch."

"You wouldn't dare."

"Try me." He was a man of his word. Macie knew that.

Her expression lost some of its playfulness. "I don't know why."

That answer felt relatively sincere, but Macie did way too much thinking for him to believe she hadn't come up with a theory or seventeen over the years. "Try to piece it out. You're gorgeous, loving, generous and a hoot. I find it hard to believe there wasn't a single man in your past who didn't see those things. Surely there was some first love. Who did you lose your virginity to?"

Macie made a disgusted face. "Oh God. The lost-virginity thing sure as hell wasn't first love. It was sort of a tipsy-at-a-party kind of thing."

"Your first time was a one-night stand?"

"Oh no. We were seventeen, which meant while the first time happened because of lowered inhibitions, we were inexperienced enough to think that might transfer over to a relationship. Believe me, the sex was a lot better after three beers."

As he tried to process that, Macie filled the silence, trying to help him understand. "So basically, my first time was a two-night stand. Nice guy, but no fireworks. He's the mayor these days."

"You lost your virginity to Philip Sanders?"

She grimaced. "Yeah. He's a total stick-in-the-mud now. Back then, he was," she paused, then grinned, "mildly interesting. It was his party. His parents were out of town and it was his one big act of rebellion. He got caught, of course, and after that, he was dull as dirt."

"Are there any guys who got beyond the second date?"

Macie nodded. "Oh yeah. Sure. Two of them. I went out with Toby Peterson for a couple of weeks when I was twenty-five."

"The assistant principal at the high school?"

"Yep. He's a super nice guy, but he has zero sense of humor."

"Okay. And the second guy?"

"He was the previous record holder before you. I dated Marcus Milhon."

"The guy from Maris who went on to become a rodeo star?"

"I had the biggest crush on him growing up. He came home one spring after a nasty fall to recuperate. Let's just say he wasn't bedridden alone for three of those weeks."

"Why did it end?"

"He went back out on the circuit. He asked me to come along, but I'm not a buckle bunny."

"And that's it?"

She smiled sadly. "It is if you don't count me proposing to Johnnie Mills."

"Harley's brother?" Her friend in the wheelchair. Everyone in Maris knew who Johnnie Mills was, had heard the story of him being thrown off the back of his dad's motorcycle when he was eleven, how he'd been paralyzed from the neck down.

He was the man who had died last year around the same time as Sharon.

Her face was sad as she nodded, and Hank figured out she had lied about never being in love. Apparently, there had been one man in her past who'd broken her heart. "Yeah. I asked him to marry me once."

"What did he say?"

"He turned me down. Said he was too much man for me." Her eyes were far away, and Hank knew she was seeing the conversation as she replayed it for him. "We had a weekly date at the restaurant for nearly six years. He'd come in and talk as I worked behind the bar."

"What did you talk about?"

"Everything. Johnnie was one of the smartest guys I ever knew. And funny as shit. And so damn sweet. I've never known anyone like him. I mean he got dealt a crappy hand, but he was never down about it. He was just this really beautiful soul."

"So you proposed?"

"I loved him." She blinked away tears and Hank could see she truly had. "So a couple years ago, I told him we should get hitched. He laughed at first, and then he figured out I was serious. Honestly, until I said the words, I hadn't realized how serious I was. Once I said it, I wanted it. Badly."

"But he said no."

"He was really kind about it. He made the joke about being too much man for me, but when I kept pressing him, he told me he loved me too much to..." She sniffled and swallowed heavily. Hank grasped her hand and squeezed it consolingly.

"Too much to...?" he prompted.

"To condemn me to a lifetime as caregiver. We kind of got into a fight after that. No matter what I said, I couldn't sway him. He left and didn't come back the next week, or the week after that. Then, three weeks after the argument, he rolled back into the restaurant and we picked up like nothing had ever happened. And I let him because I'd missed him so much it hurt. I didn't want to say anything that would make him stay away again. He died not quite a year later. Part of me has wondered since then if he knew his days were numbered. If somehow he had a sense that he wouldn't live much longer."

Suddenly he understood how so many years could have gone by without Macie settling down. She'd given her heart to Johnnie. Then he wondered how different things would be right now if Johnnie had said yes to her proposal.

"What's your dream wedding, Whiskey?"

She perked up, clearly grateful for the change of subject. He was amazed by her strength, by her ability to pull herself together and keep moving.

"That's easy. I'm eloping. In Vegas."

Hank groaned. "You're kidding, right?"

She raised her eyebrows and pointed at a face that was the very definition of serious as shit. "Do I look like I'm kidding?"

"Have you ever been to Vegas?"

She shook her head. "Nope. But a trip to Sin City is number one on my bucket list. It's that name. It inspires all sorts of fun. Have you been to Vegas?"

"No," he admitted. Unlike her, that city held very little appeal for him. "Out of curiosity, what's number two on your bucket list?"

"Officiating a lesbian wedding."

He grinned. "Well, at least you can check that one off in the near future."

He expected her to laugh, but she sobered up. "Yeah. Hopefully."

"Still struggling to write the ceremony?"

"It's freaking harder than you would think. I mean, this is *only* one of the biggest days of their lives. What I say matters. I really don't want to screw it up."

"You won't, Whiskey. Just speak from the heart and it'll be perfect."

Porter stepped onto the porch. "Sorry to bother you two. Mama Cow is in labor out in the south pasture. Looks like a breach. You're better at handling that, Coop."

Hank rose from the swing. "Okay. I'm not sure how long I'll be, Mace."

"No worries," she said. "I'll be here."

He leaned down to kiss her. "Or better yet, you could be naked in bed," he murmured.

"Go take care of that poor cow," she said, laughing as she shooed him away.

Hank hopped into the passenger side of the ranch truck, waving to her as he and Porter headed out to the south pasture. As they pulled away, he considered her bucket list.

Maybe Vegas wasn't such a bad place to visit after all.

MACIE HAD JUST SHUT down the TV an hour later when headlights flashed through the window and along the living room wall. Rather than strip down to nothing, Macie had donned a brand new sexy nightie she'd bought herself on a whim, while out shopping for wedding stuff with Amanda the previous weekend. She struck a sexy pose on the coffee table and waited for Hank to come in.

She was surprised when there was a knock at the door. Hank wouldn't knock. Neither would Porter. A quick glance at the clock told her it was just after nine. Which felt a bit late for a social call.

Macie had changed in the bedroom and come down in nothing but this damn scrap of lace.

"A smart person would have put on a robe," she muttered as she looked around the living room for something to cover herself up with. She couldn't walk upstairs because to get there required walking by the front door—and its clear glass window that gave the visitor the perfect view inside.

"To hell with it." She grabbed a fleece blanket and draped it over her shoulders, clutching it together in front. It didn't cover as much of her legs as she liked, but she figured she revealed at least that much at the lake in the summer.

As she walked to the door, she was relieved to see Janice standing outside. She opened the door with a smile. "Thank goodness, Janice. I was afraid it was one of the ranch hands. As you can see, I'm all by my lonesome and not exactly dressed for company."

Macie stepped aside as Janice entered. "Coop's not here?"

Macie shook her head. "No. He's out in one of the pastures delivering a breach calf. No telling what time he'll get back."

"Oh." Janice looked disappointed to hear that and once again, Macie felt sorry for the woman. Like Janice, Macie knew how much it hurt to lose a close friend. Johnnie's death had left a gaping hole inside her, and she figured the same held true for Janice.

"You want to have some tea or a glass of wine or something?"

Janice appeared surprised by the invitation and Macie wondered why. She didn't think she'd ever slighted the woman. Hell, she hardly knew Janice. Like Hank, Janice was older, so their paths never crossed growing up. And Janice lived with her elderly parents, caring for them, so it wasn't like they ran into each other at social events either. As far as Macie knew, Janice didn't go out much.

"Tea would be nice."

Macie gestured toward the kitchen, sorry Janice hadn't picked wine. And then sorry she'd suggested the damn tea. She really felt like wine, but guessed it would be rude to pour herself a glass of vino instead of having tea with her guest. She hated adulting.

She poured them each a glass of iced tea as Janice sat at the table.

"So, what's new?" Macie asked, when it was clear Janice wasn't going to start the conversation.

"Not much. My mother fell and sprained her wrist a couple days ago."

"Oh no. I'm sorry to hear that."

Janice shrugged. "She'll be okay. Your cousin, Tyson, wrapped it up for her."

Macie wasn't sure if she was being oversensitive or if she was genuinely detecting a tone of disgust in Janice's voice when she mentioned Tyson's name. Ever since Tyson's unusual relationship with Harley and Caleb came out, the trio had been dealing with some fallout from the judgmental assholes in Maris.

"Tyson is a great doctor. Your mom was in good hands."

Janice's smirk and dismissive *hmpf* proved Macie wasn't imagining things. And just like that, her willingness to play the good hostess dried up. Nothing got Macie's back up quicker than someone insulting her family.

She pushed her glass of tea aside and reached for a wineglass. "Did you stop by for a reason? Is there something I can do for you instead? I'm really not sure how long Hank will be gone."

"Why do you call him Hank?"

The question took Macie aback, even though it wasn't the first time it had been posed. A couple of her cousins and her sister had remarked on it when she and Hank first started dating. "He asked me to."

Janice frowned. "Why?"

Macie sat across the table from Janice and took a quick sip of her wine. "I don't really know why. I assume it's because he thinks it would be weird for his girlfriend to call him by his last name."

"Sharon called him Coop."

Macie hadn't expected that. She'd figured Hank's request had been based on the fact he missed hearing his first name from his wife. "Oh." Macie wasn't sure how else to reply to that and Janice wasn't someone she felt comfortable sharing confidences with anyway.

Janice gestured toward her blanket. "Are you living here now?"

Macie tried to decide if Janice was just making conversation or if this was some sort of third degree. "No, I haven't moved in." And then, because there was something in Janice's gaze that tweaked her, Macie added, "Yet."

That word seemed to take the wind out of Janice's sails. "Do you expect Coop to propose to you?"

Janice's tone wasn't rude, in fact all her questions were posed in a very sweet voice. Even so, Macie found her annoyance growing with each prying question. Her personal life really wasn't any of Janice's business.

"We've only been dating a month."

Janice nodded as if that was somehow the correct answer. Like there were right or wrong responses. Macie took a bigger drink of wine, not missing the way Janice watched her actions closely.

She was sorry she'd given Janice a full glass of tea. She was ready for the woman to leave.

"Do you like to cook, Macie?"

Macie was getting whiplash from this woman's questions. "No. Not at all. I'm actually a disaster when it comes to making anything edible."

Again, Janice seemed pleased by her answer. So she was two for two in this weird quiz. Macie wondered what the grand prize at the end would be.

"I see. Sharon and I both loved to cook. We spent a great deal of time in this kitchen, fixing meals for Coop and Porter and the other hands. And I can't begin to count the number of meals I've brought over to Coop in the last year."

Macie toyed with the stem of her glass. "That was neighborly of you." Macie wondered how many he'd eaten, given the fact he was in the restaurant most nights, chowing down on the daily special.

"I suppose you'll take over the restaurant business from your father when he decides to retire."

Macie nodded slowly. That was the plan. And pretty much everybody in Maris knew that. "Yeah. With Adele." And her cousins.

"Work must take up a great deal of your time."

It used to. Simply because Macie was a people person and it wasn't like she'd had that much going on in her real life. As such, she'd worked longer hours behind the bar because—sad as it sounded—it had been her happy place. In the last month, that had changed completely. Her new happy place was anywhere Hank was. "The hours aren't terrible and they're pretty flexible."

"Even so, you have to admit that having a full-time job and being a rancher's wife would be extremely difficult."

Ah. Gotcha. Macie worked overtime not to roll her eyes. Janice didn't approve of Hank's new girlfriend. No doubt she felt she owed it to Sharon to make sure her husband found someone more suitable to date.

Shit like this fired Macie up. Two could play the Janice game, so Macie put on her sweetest smile and when she spoke, it was like pure sugar dripping out of her mouth. "Oh, I don't think it would be that hard at all. The ranch hands fend for themselves these days. Hank and I take dinner alone together, and he's a wonderful cook."

"You make him cook?"

Hello, Miss 1950. Way to set women back sixty years.

"*Make* him? No. I don't tie him to the stove. He likes to cook."

"Coop never made dinner when Sharon was alive."

"I see." It was on the tip of her tongue to remind Janice that Sharon *wasn't* alive, but no matter how pissed off Macie was, she wouldn't—couldn't—be so cruel.

"I just think perhaps you've got blinders on where Coop is concerned, Macie. The poor man lost the love of his life. He's not exactly thinking clearly. I'm sure the two of you have fun together." Janice's gaze dropped to where Macie's blanket had fallen open to reveal her nightie. Macie tightened her grip on the fleece.

"He's a man. And he has needs. But you have to see that in the long run, the two of you aren't compatible. Beyond the physical, he needs a wife to cook, clean and run this home, to take care of him."

Macie's blood was boiling. She was so fucking angry, she could hardly see straight. "I think you should leave."

Janice had the gall to look affronted, like Macie had insulted her. The woman had just looked Macie in the eye and all but called her a slut, whose only purpose in Hank's life was to spread her legs for the grieving widower, and *she* had the nerve to act slighted.

"Macie, I'm not saying these things to be unkind. Surely you see that Coop is trying to find his sea legs again. Trying to move on without Sharon. He's going to make a few mistakes along the way and I'd hate to see you get hurt."

So now Macie was a mistake? A slut *and* a mistake? Macie had never hit another person in her life, but if Janice didn't get away from her in the next thirty seconds, that record was going to end in brutal fashion.

"Janice, my personal life is none of your concern. At all. And now, I'd like you to leave before I call my *other* cousin, Evan, the cop, to drag you out of here."

Janice rose, shaking her head and giving Macie a holier-than-thou look that insinuated she might have expected such behavior.

Macie balled her hand in a fist and started counting to ten.

Mercifully, Janice moved toward the kitchen door. Before she left, she looked over her shoulder at Macie. "You may be angry at me, Macie, but I think if you dig deep, you'll realize that you're not Coop's type. Sharon was. And you're not her. You never will be."

With that, Janice left.

And Macie picked up her wineglass and threw it against a wall.

Sinking back into her chair, it took a full five minutes for Macie to stop trembling with anger. And another twenty minutes before she managed to stop muttering aloud all the things she wished she'd said to Janice.

Why did the zingers always come after the fact? Shit like that just pissed her off even more.

After thirty minutes, Macie had calmed down enough to stand and clean the broken glass. Then she called Amanda. The two of them cussed Janice VanMeter up one side and down the other—because that was what friends did. Amanda was the best at righteous indignation, never failing to leap to Macie's defense when needed. Once she'd had a good long bitch session, she and Amanda said goodbye.

And an hour later, she was alone in Hank's bed. And trying to drown out the one thing Janice had said that stuck, no matter how much Macie tried to forget it.

You're not Coop's type. Sharon was.

Macie had said that exact same thing at the beginning. And Hank had assured her she was being silly. He had assured her so well, she'd believed him, but the truth was, Macie was his first relationship since Sharon's death. She had watched enough damn chick flicks to know about the transition girlfriend. There was always a chance that was what she was. The woman to help Hank heal, to help him move on with his life.

And then...he'd move on.

To someone more his type. Someone closer to his age, who could cook. Who wanted to be a full-time rancher's wife. Who didn't talk constantly, cuss like a sailor, drink too much, tell dirty jokes and gossip shamelessly. Someone who was calm and quiet and well versed in being a grown-up and a lady.

Someone like Sharon. Whom he'd loved dearly.

Macie looked at the clock and wished Hank would hurry up and get back. Lying in bed alone was giving her too much time to think.

And the worst part was she'd let Janice get to her. She was smarter than that. She knew the woman had said those things to be cruel. But damn if the bitch hadn't found the weak spot, hadn't cut the right artery.

Because Macie *had been* struggling with the ghost of

Sharon, comparing herself to the woman, worrying about measuring up.

She and Hank had amazing sex, there was no denying that. And they had fun together. But was that enough?

Her cell phone pinged. She glanced at the screen, surprised to see Porter's name.

On way back. Coop's phone died. He wanted you to be ready.

She grinned, despite the heavy feeling in her chest. She knew what *be ready* meant.

Then she recalled Porter's presence in the kitchen last week as he watched her and Hank. Sharon had taken them both to her bed. And it was obvious Hank had enjoyed that aspect of their sex life. He'd mentioned it to her the first week they'd started dating.

Macie's heart began to race as she considered her next move. Realistically, she knew she wasn't in a very good frame of mind. So what she was thinking of doing was really stupid. But she also wasn't sure she'd ever have the courage to initiate this in a lucid state.

Having Porter watch them had been really hot. Maybe taking it to the next level would...what? Make the current mess bigger? Make things clearer? Make it obvious that she could be just as good for Hank as Sharon was?

What the fuck was her goal?

She sucked at planning. And common sense.

So before she could reconsider, she responded to Porter's text.

You coming with him?

There was no reply, even though she could see Porter had

read the thing. God. No doubt the men were sitting in the truck thinking WTF right about now.

She stood up, pacing the floor and trying to give herself a pep talk.

"You're better than this, Macie," she mumbled. "You're letting that bitch win. Get her out of your head. You *are* his type. Hank's crazy about you. You're crazy about him. You can do this. You can do this. He loves you. He loves you. He loves you."

"He loves you."

She twisted at the sound of Hank's voice in the doorway. Shit. How long had he been there? Given his amused grin, she was fairly certain he hadn't heard it all. Otherwise, he would have asked who the bitch was.

"Hey."

He tilted his head as his gaze raked over her, taking in her nightie. "You okay?"

She nodded. "Yes."

"Nervous?"

Stressed-out was probably a better description, but when Hank stepped into the room, followed by Porter, she knew he'd misinterpreted her pacing and muttering.

Hank's forehead creased when she didn't reply, when her mouth fell open and she made a very unattractive squeaking noise.

He frowned. "Yeah. That's what I thought. Macie, I don't think this is a good idea."

"No," she called out quickly. She needed to take some sort of control back. Needed to reclaim the confidence she'd let Janice shake. "Wait."

"No, we're not waiting." She didn't have a clue what Hank saw in her face, but obviously her pep talk hadn't worked.

Hank glanced at Porter, who walked toward her. He cupped her cheek and gave her a soft kiss. Macie stood stock-still through it all, confused as hell. And panicking. She thought by "not waiting," they weren't going ahead.

But now they were?

Oh God. What would they do if she screamed and ran out of the room?

Porter smiled at her. "Me and Coop talked. This isn't going to work out, Macie."

She blinked rapidly, fairly certain she hadn't taken a breath in the last five minutes. "What?"

"I'll let him explain it to you, but I just wanted to tell you that I think you're beautiful and I'm very flattered that you'd even consider taking me back to your bed after the last time, but—"

"The last time wasn't bad." The words fell out of her mouth without her thinking about them. Like that was anything new.

Hank chuckled, while Porter grinned. "Thanks for that. I think you and me are going to be really good friends."

With that, he gave her a wink and left the room.

"Hank, I—"

"I can't share you. Not even with Porter." His admission took her by surprise.

"I don't understand. You and Sharon—"

"You're not Sharon, Macie. And I was wrong to...God, to think you were."

His words went through her like a knife, but she schooled her features, refused to let him see how hurt she was.

"You sent that text, inviting Porter upstairs, and I knew I'd kill him if he touched you." Hank crossed the room, guilt covering his features as he took her hands in his. "I hope you can forgive me. I told you there was nothing I wouldn't give you if it was possible, but letting another man near you, well... that's not going to happen."

Nothing he said was making sense to her. She wasn't Sharon, but suddenly that didn't seem like a bad thing. "You're jealous of Porter?"

"Yeah. Insanely so. I didn't intend to fall so fast, Whiskey. I spent twenty years of my life in love with the same woman, and I made the mistake of thinking that all love felt the same. I was a fool."

She processed that and realized he was right. She'd genuinely loved Johnnie, but her feelings for him were night and day compared to what she felt for Hank. "I get it. And I've been acting like an idiot tonight too. I thought if I asked Porter up here, it would prove to you that I could take Sharon's place."

Hank scowled. "I don't want you to take her place. I want *you*. Just you. The way you are. Dammit, Macie. Are you saying you would have slept with a man you didn't want just to please me?"

She shook her head. "No. I'm pretty sure it wouldn't have gotten that far. I was contemplating running from the house like the hounds of hell were nipping at my heels when Porter walked over to me."

"Pretty sure?"

Leave it to Hank to latch on to the wrong part. His hands were on his hips and the man was seriously ticked off.

"Hank," she said, reaching out to run her hands along his chest.

He gripped her wrists, tugging them away and pulling them behind her back. Her body responded instantly. As always.

Clenching pussy, tight nipples, racing heart, trouble breathing.

If she put those symptoms in WebMD, the only disease on her list would be Hank Cooper.

"Macie—" he started.

"I wouldn't have slept with him."

He studied her face for a full minute, and then he released her hands.

"I like this nightie," he said as he gripped the neckline and tore the sheer lace in half, dropping his destruction to the floor.

She glanced down and shook her head. "You owe me thirty bucks."

He didn't reply. Instead, he turned her, backing her up until her legs hit the bed. Then with pressure on her shoulder, he pushed her to the mattress, coming over her.

"You're still dressed." It was her most common complaint. Hank was very good at getting her out of her clothes, but he lost all patience when it came to shedding his own. Typically he just bared the essentials. And when that happened, she forgot to complain about the rest.

"Mmmhmmm," he murmured as his lips trailed along her chest, between her breasts, moving lower. He pressed her legs apart, kneeling between them. He stroked her clit with his tongue as he pushed two fingers inside her.

And just like that, Macie forgot about his fully dressed state again. Using his tongue, fingers and teeth, he dragged one orgasm out of her and got her damn close to the second before rising to shrug off his jeans and kick off his shoes. To her surprise, he even pulled off his shirt.

"Get in the middle of the bed, Whiskey. I don't want to fuck you tonight."

She scowled and started to assure him there was no way in hell they weren't having sex, but he just dragged her where he wanted her.

"I'm making love to you."

"Oh."

Her legs opened and then he was there, sliding inside her. He rocked in and out, the two of them swaying like a boat on a placid lake. Throughout it all, he whispered so many perfect things, she felt certain she was dreaming.

"You're so beautiful."

"God, I love you."

"How did I live a second without you, Whiskey?"

"Want you in my bed every night."

As they reached their climaxes, he kissed her softly. Macie went over first, but Hank was only seconds behind. Then he withdrew, moved behind her and spooned her as he fell asleep within minutes.

Macie lay there listening to his slow, deep breathing and every bad thought, every anxiety she'd suffered, simply drifted away.

CHAPTER SEVEN

HANK WALKED INTO HIS KITCHEN, took one look around and wondered if he'd been robbed.

"Macie?" he yelled out. Silence answered him. He'd spent the entire day in Douglas at a stock sale and had called earlier to say he was running late. At the time, he noticed Macie sounded flustered.

Stepping into the room, he tried to take stock of the disaster surrounding him. There was a scorched skillet soaking in the sink that was never going to be saved. The stench of burned meat assaulted his nose. He followed it to the trashcan under the sink, where he discovered a huge pile of black...something. Maybe chicken.

There was flour all over the counters, the floor and the table, and in the midst of the sea of white was a very flat pancake-looking thing in a cake pan. Next to it was some concoction that looked like butter, sugar, milk and food coloring. He didn't have a clue what that was supposed to be.

There were lumpy mashed potatoes in a pot, raw broccoli in a bowl and a half-drunk bottle of wine.

Concerned when she didn't appear, he dug out his cell phone and called her. And was instantly greeted by her ring tone, "It's Five O'Clock Somewhere," coming from beneath a pile of sticky paper towels on the counter. The woman was infamous for leaving her phone behind. Most of the time, he thought it was funny. Right now, it was frustrating.

"Whoa. What happened in here?" Porter asked as he stepped into the kitchen.

"That's what I'm trying to figure out."

When Porter looked around and mumbled a curse, Hank looked his way for an answer. "You figured it out?"

Porter nodded. "It's your birthday."

"I know." And the light went on. "Macie tried to make me dinner."

"And a cake, I think," Porter said, pointing to the pancake and blue milk in a bowl. "I might've mentioned how Sharon always went all out for your birthday. Home-cooked dinner, cake, presents."

Hank closed his eyes and sighed. "I wish you hadn't done that."

"I didn't realize her skills were quite this...I mean...shit, man, she works in a restaurant."

"As the bartender. And she's sort of sensitive about Sharon comparisons. She feels like she needs to compete or measure up or something." Hank thought he'd talked her off that ledge last week after delivering the cow, but given her efforts tonight, he feared there was still some convincing to do.

"She what?" Porter asked. "Why does she think she needs to compete with Sharon? Macie's awesome the way she is."

Hank grinned. His best friend was definitely starting to come around after his initial assessment of Macie. "I know. And I've told her that. More than once."

"Guess I can't blame her really," Porter said after a moment's contemplation.

"What do you mean?"

"You and Sharon were the perfect couple, happy, in love, devoted. It's kind of a tough act to follow."

"It's not like I'm holding up a measuring stick or keeping notes about who did what better. I love Macie for who she is. I'm not worried about who she isn't."

Porter looked around the kitchen. "I'm thinking that's a good thing. Because damn, man, you can't ever let her loose in here again."

"Yeah. That's a given. Doesn't help me figure out where she is now."

"Knowing Macie, when she realized she'd lost the battle with," Porter pointed to the charred meat in the trashcan, "whatever that poor creature was, she probably went in search of other food."

The light went on for both of them at the same time. "Sparks Barbeque," they said in unison.

"I'll fire up the truck," Porter offered.

"You don't have to run into town with me."

Porter shrugged. "I know, but it's that or breathe in this noxious, scorched air. Might grab my own dinner while I'm there."

Twenty minutes later, the two of them had parked the truck. One quick glance around the parking lot told Hank her car wasn't there. "Maybe we missed her."

"Only one way to find out," Porter said, climbing out of the truck. "Let's go inside and ask."

"What are you doing here?" Sydney asked two seconds after he and Porter walked into the restaurant.

"I'm looking for Macie," Hank said, spotting Amanda and Brandi sitting at the counter. From the looks on their faces, he could tell they were surprised to see him too. Apparently Macie had shared her plans for his birthday with everyone. Not that he should be shocked by that. The woman wasn't known for keeping her thoughts to herself.

"She's at your place, isn't she?" Brandi asked.

Hank shook his head. "No. The only thing at my place is a bunch of burned food and a path of destruction unlike any I've ever seen before."

Sydney laughed. "I told her fried chicken was tough and she was going to have to concentrate."

"Yeah," Hank sighed. "It definitely went south, and now she's not there. I can only assume she got upset when everything went to hell and took off. Any idea where she would go?"

"It's Macie," Adele said as she wiped the counter. "She could be anywhere. Did you try to call her?"

"Yeah. She left her cell behind."

Adele laughed. "God, I don't even know why she owns a phone. She never remembers to carry the damn thing anywhere."

Amanda patted Hank on the shoulder. "Don't worry. Once she calms down, she'll come back."

"Does she run away often?" he asked, unable to shake the feeling that didn't sound much like Macie.

Amanda shook her head. "No. Never. But she's never really been in love like this before. She wanted today to be special. Knowing her, once plan A failed, she went out in search of plan B."

"Oh yeah. It's probably plan B," Adele said in agreement.

"What was plan B?" Hank asked.

Adele shrugged though it was apparent she had a hunch.

"Where is she, Addie?" Porter asked.

Hank looked up, surprised by his friend's overly familiar tone with Macie's sister.

"I hate that nickname," Adele said, arms crossed. "And I told you. I don't know. Besides, this is all *your* fault anyway. Telling Macie about how special Sharon made Coop's birthday every year and how he didn't celebrate it last year without her."

"You told her that too?" Hank asked, exasperated. Clearly, Macie had felt a great deal of pressure to make the day perfect. And given the current state of his kitchen, she was upset at failing.

Before Porter could answer, Adele's phone beeped with an incoming text. She snickered.

"Macie?" Hank asked.

Adele nodded. "Yeah. She wants me to swing by KFC to pick up a bucket and deliver it to your place."

"So she's back at the ranch?"

Adele grinned. "I'm gonna say yes, since that's where her phone is."

Hank chuckled. "Shit. Yeah. Forgot about that. Don't worry about the chicken, Adele. I'll grab some on the way home. Save you a trip."

Adele groaned. "She's going to hate that. She really did want your birthday to be perfect."

"It'll be fine." Hank was touched by Macie's efforts.

The bell over the door to the restaurant rang and Macie's aunt, Beverly walked in with a box. "Hey, Adele. Macie wants you to take this cake out to the ranch. It's for..." She spotted Hank standing there. "What are you doing here?"

Hank grinned and pointed to the box. "My birthday cake?"

Beverly looked as if she wanted to lie, but in the end, she just handed it to him. "Happy Birthday. Hope you like chocolate."

Hank accepted the box. "I love it. We better get rolling, Porter. I don't want to be late to my birthday supper."

Porter rolled his eyes. "The one you're buying? Why don't you head on back? I'll catch a ride with Addie later."

Adele scowled. "No, you won't. I don't live anywhere near the ranch."

Porter appeared to ignore her words. "What time do you get off, Addie?

Adele threw up her hand. "I'm not talking to you as long as you persist in calling me that. And I'm sure as hell not driving you home."

She walked back to the kitchen and, to Hank's amazement, Porter started to follow her. "Catch you later, Coop."

Hank's curiosity about Porter and Adele was short-lived, his excitement about his birthday dinner growing. He hopped in his truck, swung through the drive-thru at the KFC for a bucket, and then headed home.

Macie's car was parked in its usual spot when he arrived.

He wasn't two steps in the front door when he heard her in the kitchen. From the sounds of things, she hadn't finished the cleanup.

When he walked into the kitchen, he realized she hadn't made much headway at all. At least ninety percent of the disaster he'd witnessed earlier remained.

"Shit," she said when she looked up and spotted him. Then she saw the bucket of chicken and the cake box in his hands. "Where did you get that?"

"I was at the restaurant when you texted Adele and your aunt. Told them I'd save them a trip."

His response appeared to be the last straw.

Macie sank down in a chair and bowed her head, exhaustion and frustration taking over. "Shit." Her voice broke. She was near tears.

Hank set the food down on the table and knelt in front of her. "Hey now. Don't do that, Whiskey. This is the perfect birthday surprise."

She glanced up at that, almost sneering. "Oh yeah. Just perfect." She gestured at the destroyed kitchen. "I burned the chicken. The mashed potatoes are chunky and sort of raw. And I don't have a fucking clue what happened to that cake. The kitchen's a wreck. I owe you a skillet, by the way."

He lifted one shoulder casually, trying very hard not to laugh. "I still owe you a nightie, so we'll call it even."

"Sharon gave you perfect birthdays. All I've given you is a gigantic mess."

"Stop it. I don't ever want to hear you compare yourself to her again. It's not a competition, Macie. Jesus. You're you and she was her. You're not the same woman, and I sure as hell don't want or expect you to be."

"You would think you being sweet about this would help, but it doesn't. Just makes me feel worse." She sniffled. "You even had to buy your own dinner. And it's in a bucket, not on nice plates. Just feels like I'm not really cut out for this."

"For what?"

"Ranch life. I mean, what do I contribute around here? I can't cook for the hands or you. There are more wrinkles in a shirt *after* I iron it than before. And I typically get my apartment cleaned through blackmail."

"Blackmail?"

"Adele's no angel."

Hank didn't bother to hide his grin anymore, which only served to tweak Macie even more. Clearly she thought he was laughing at her.

"Anything else?" he asked, deciding it was probably good that they got all this out on the table now. He wasn't sure what had gotten her so down on herself, but he'd noticed a definite change in the last week or so. Given her usual overabundance of confidence, he hated seeing her questioning her worth.

"I'm not overly fond of horses. Or cows—lot of flies come with those damn cows. I grew up in town, so I'm used to streetlights. It gets really fucking dark out here. Like, unnaturally dark."

"So you don't want to live on the ranch?"

Her eyes widened. "I didn't say that. I just said I didn't grow up like this. I'm pretty sure there are things I should—or could—be doing to pitch in that I don't even know about. Like," she waved her hand around, "mucking a stall or something."

"You want to clean up horse shit?"

She crinkled her nose. "Christ, no. I'm just making a point. And you're being contrary on purpose."

Hank got up from the floor, dragging a chair over so he could sit close to her. "You're right. I am. Because nothing you're saying makes sense. I pay ranch hands to muck the stalls. I'm not dating you because I want a housekeeper or a cook. I could pay somebody to do that too. Or, like you said, I could just blackmail your sister. By the way, what's going on with Adele and Porter?"

"I have no idea. It started a few days ago."

"Are they fighting?"

She shrugged. "I think it looks a lot like sexual tension. Which is weird because I didn't think they ever really talked to each other beyond her taking his order at the restaurant."

"Yeah." The squirrel he'd tossed in her path only distracted her for a minute. Then she looked around the kitchen again, and he could see fresh tears filling her pretty brown eyes.

"Macie. Don't cry. I mean it. There's nothing here to cry about. This is probably one of the best birthdays I've ever had."

"You're just being nice."

"No. I'm not. You can't cook and you know that. Even so,

you stepped way out of your comfort zone to try it. For me. That's one of the nicest things anybody's ever done for me, Whiskey."

"I thought after last year's birthday..."

"Porter really filled you in on everything, didn't he?"

"I asked."

"I got wasted. Locked myself in the living room and fell into a bottle of whiskey. Not my brightest move. Paid for it with the mother of all hangovers for two days after."

"That's why I wanted to make sure this year was different."

He cupped her cheek and then, because he couldn't resist her a second longer, he kissed her. "You did, believe me."

He grinned and she rolled her eyes.

"I meant different in a good way. All this room makes me want to do is fall into my *own* bottle of bourbon."

"That's funny. I look around and feel really good. Every single thing in here shows me how much you care about me. And that is the best gift a man could ever get."

Macie softened in his arms, and he sensed some of the tension seeping out of her. He hoped—prayed—that he'd set her mind at ease once and for all.

Then he realized he knew exactly how to relax her even more. He kissed her again, letting his hands drift to her breasts.

The second he touched her, she gasped. "Oh! Your gift! I forgot."

He tightened his grip on her. "The only thing I want to unwrap right now is you, in my bed."

She shrugged off his hold and hopped up quickly. "This can't wait. Sorry." She darted across the kitchen to the mudroom in the back. She opened the door and bent down to pick something up.

When she turned around, she had a squirming puppy in her arms. Around its neck, she'd tied a big red bow.

Hank was speechless as she returned to him.

"Porter said you love dogs, but you never had one because Sharon was deathly afraid of them. Said something about her being bitten when she was younger."

"You got me a puppy?"

She bit her lip. "That was stupid, wasn't it? Pets are horrible presents, I know that. I mean, God, I just saddled you with a bunch of work, and they're expensive and—"

"You got me a puppy," he repeated.

"Yeah. Sorry."

"Is it a boy or a girl?"

"A girl. That's where I was when you came home and found the mess. I was supposed to pick her up earlier, but Rodney was late getting home from his granddaughter's birthday party in Douglas."

"Can I hold her?"

Macie held the wiggly dog out to him. "Of course you can. She's yours...if you want to keep her."

The second the puppy was in his arms, Hank fell in love. The dog tried to climb his chest and suddenly his face was covered with sloppy kisses as she licked every part of him she could reach. Hank laughed and realized Macie really had given him the best birthday ever.

"What's her name?" he asked.

"She doesn't have one yet."

He looked at the sweet dog and studied her face. "Sally. She looks like a Sally."

Macie stared at the dog, then shrugged. "Yeah. I guess she kind of does. So, you like her?"

"I love her. Jesus, Mace. This is..." He swallowed, surprised by the lump that had formed in his throat. This time last year, he'd been in the darkest place imaginable. Alone, angry at the world.

This year, he had the sweetest, silliest, sexiest woman giving him puppies and making him laugh and burning his favorite dinner.

"This is perfect. All of it."

He wasn't sure what she saw in his face or heard in his tone, but for the first time since he'd walked into the kitchen, she appeared to believe what he was saying.

"She's adorable, isn't she? I mean she's a mutt, part black lab, part whodunit. Rodney said she'll probably get pretty big."

"Macie?"

"Yeah?"

"Get upstairs. Now."

She giggled. "What about the chicken?"

"Take the bucket with you. We'll eat it cold, in bed, after."

Macie picked up the KFC bucket and headed for the stairs. Hank considered putting the puppy down for all of two seconds, and then decided to bring her along. He wasn't quite ready to put the sweet girl down yet.

Macie narrowed her eyes when they reached the top of

the stairs. "You're going to be one of those people who spoils his pet beyond reason, aren't you?"

Hank grinned. "Yep."

"Dog in the bed with us?"

He laughed as they entered his bedroom. "Only when we're sleeping."

Macie rolled her eyes. "You heard the part about Sally being a big dog, right?"

Hank tossed an extra blanket on the floor, creating a makeshift dog bed for Sally. The puppy crawled onto it and laid down, her chin on her paws as she sleepily watched the two of them.

"I'll buy a bigger bed. Figure we'll need one once kids come along anyway."

Though it didn't happen often, every now and again, Hank was able to render Macie speechless...for a few seconds.

"That was a hell of a leap."

"Told you from the beginning where we were headed, Whiskey. My goals haven't changed. If anything, I'm anxious to jump to the next part. This past month with you has only made me greedy for more."

"Like *kids* more?"

He nodded. "I'm not getting any younger, Mace. In fact, as of today, I'm another year older. Forty-two. I'd like to have babies while I'm still able to pick them up." Hank hadn't intended to bring up this conversation, but seeing the squirming puppy in Macie's arms downstairs had fired up a mess of desires he'd kept on the back burner for most of his life.

Hank wanted to be a father. Wanted to have kids with Macie.

"When do you get your next birth control shot?"

Macie's forehead creased as she did some mental calculations. "Um..." Apparently the date clicked and she winced. "I was due last week."

"Don't get it."

"You're insane. We've dated one month, Hank. If this is some sort of midlife crisis, brought on by the birthday and the puppy, then I think you need to take a couple steps back and think a little harder on all of this. We're still working out the relationship bumps."

"What bumps?"

Macie's nose crinkled adorably as she clearly tried to come up with something. "Well." She paused, and then, because she obviously couldn't think of anything, she raised her hands as if she'd proven some point. "And there you have it. The fact that there haven't been any proves that this is still the honeymoon phase. You can't make life-altering decisions in the midst of all this amazing sex. You gotta let it get old, have a few fights."

"So we can't discuss having kids until we're sick of sex and pissed off at each other?"

She lifted one shoulder. She appeared to realize how silly that sounded, but Macie never backed down easy. "Uhhhh... yeah. Exactly."

"Whiskey?" Hank said, stepping close enough he could grasp her waist with his hands.

"Yeah?"

"I'm never going to get sick of fucking you. And I'm

pretty sure there's nothing you could do that would piss me off for long."

She chuckled. "Give me time."

"I want to make babies with you. How long do those damn shots last?"

"The one I get lasts three months."

"Can we compromise?"

She tilted her head curiously. "How?"

"Instead of getting the shot again, how about you go on the Pill? We can take it one month at a time. Until I wear you down."

Macie grinned. "Cocky bastard. You really think you're going to win this argument, don't you?"

He nodded. "Yep." He turned her away from him, so that her back was pressed against his chest, both of them facing the bed. "Imagine the two of us in that bed, Whiskey. With a couple of squirming kids between us."

"The kids *and* the dog are going to be in the bed with us?"

"Just on nights when they're scared—if it's storming or they have a bad dream or wet the bed."

"You're going to spoil our kids as much as the damn dog."

Hank's hands tightened on her waist when she said the word *our*. Much as Macie might demur and try to play the common sense card, deep down she knew the same thing he did. Even if she struggled to admit it.

They were going to get married. They were going to have a family.

"Don't worry so much, Whiskey. I'm going to spoil you too." As he spoke, he lifted the hem of her shirt, tugging it over her head. Within seconds, she was naked, still facing away from him as he reached around to cup her breasts.

Their conversation had stirred up too many emotions in him. He took her nipples between his thumbs and index fingers and applied pressure, pinching them until she gasped.

"Hank." His name fell out on a whisper.

"Speaking of spoiling," he murmured as he kissed her bare shoulder. "Get on the bed. Hands and knees. I bought you a present."

"But it's your birthday."

"This gift is for both of us." He reached into the nightstand drawer and pulled out the vibrator that had arrived in the mail yesterday. He'd spent the weekend doing a little online sex-toy shopping while Macie had been at work.

The vibrator was just one thing he'd purchased, but he intended to introduce her to the rest of his stash one kinky night at a time.

He placed the vibrator on the bed next to her, letting her see it, letting her overactive imagination play out all the ways he'd use it on her, as he dug for the lube as well.

"I'm guessing you didn't buy condoms."

"Does the shot wear off that quickly?"

She shook her head, slowly. "No, I don't think so. I'm pretty sure it doesn't. Oh, I don't have a fucking clue. I'll call tomorrow about switching over to the Pill."

He grinned. He'd won the first battle.

Uncapping the lube, he squeezed some into her ass. Macie jerked briefly in surprise, but he'd anticipated the response. His free hand gripped her hip tightly, holding her in place as he added even more.

"Have to admit that wasn't what I'd envisioned when you put that vibrator on the bed."

Hank placed a kiss in the middle of her back. "Figured you might want a taste of what it would have been like to take two men to bed with you."

She glanced over her shoulder. "Not sure Porter would like knowing you're replacing him with that vibrator. It's not exactly," she hesitated, "big."

Hank laughed. "You'll be glad I didn't grab a bigger model in a second." Picking up the toy, he placed the tip at her anus, enjoying her shiver of arousal. Macie hadn't shied away from anything he'd done with her. To her.

Her desires seemed to match his perfectly.

Slowly, he pressed the vibrator deeper. He'd fucked her ass a few times with just his fingers. The vibrator was smooth and narrow and it slid in with ease. Macie's back arched as it went deeper, and her soft moan told him she liked the sensation.

Hell, pretty soon they were both going to enjoy the new toy. Once it was seated to the hilt, he turned the vibrator on slow.

Macie jerked again. "Oh. Oh my God."

"You like that?"

She nodded.

Hank always swore he'd go slow with her, take his time, tease and tantalize her. And he failed in that endeavor. Every time.

The image of Macie on her hands and knees with the slender toy vibrating in her sexy ass was more than he could take.

He put the head of his cock against the opening to her hot, wet pussy and shoved in. His forward thrust pushed the vibrator as well. He could feel the pulsations along the top of his dick, the sensation so overwhelming, he had to stop for a minute to suck in some much-needed air. He needed to get a grip or this was going to be over before it started.

Hank gritted his teeth, closed his eyes and fought for control, as Macie unwittingly did everything in her power to destroy him. She didn't appear to have noticed he'd stilled. How could she when the sexy minx was working overtime to grab her own pleasure?

She'd begun thrusting back and forth on his cock, her little sex sounds driving him wild. When she reached down to rub her clit, Hank realized it was time to take over before it was too late.

Gripping her wrists, he tugged them roughly behind her back. It was something he did often. One, because he loved it, and two, because it never failed to make Macie's pussy clench even tighter against him. The woman loved being restrained, rendered helpless.

His abrupt actions sent her head and upper chest down to the mattress, leaving her ass in the air. As such, his cock went in even deeper.

Hank leaned over, rummaging through the nightstand again. He'd intended to pull the toys out one by one over several nights, but he wanted both hands free tonight. Grabbing the fur-lined handcuffs he'd bought, he clicked them onto her wrists, which were still resting at the base of her back.

The new form of bondage provoked the right response.

Macie's body trembled with arousal, her inner muscles tightening down on his cock so hard he saw stars.

"Fuck, Macie. You're so sexy, baby. So fucking gorgeous."

Much as she liked to talk, in bed, she liked to listen. His words of praise worked against her own struggle for control. And when he reached around her hip to touch her clit, it was game over.

She cried out loudly as she came. Hard.

So fucking hard.

It took all the strength in his body not to follow. Once her climax waned, he held still. He pretended he was giving her time to recover, but the reprieve was all for him. He wasn't finished with her. Not by a long shot.

After a few minutes, Hank was ready. He cranked the vibrator in her ass on high, gripped her hips tightly and took her. Forcefully.

Macie's hands were clenched in fists at her back, even as she sought for some semblance of control. Somehow she managed to find a way to push back each time he thrust forward, urging him on with her moans and pleas.

God. He loved her.

"Harder," she demanded. "Fuck. Harder, Hank!"

Reaching up, he grasped a handful of her hair, tugging it to lift her chest off the bed until her bound hands were pressed tight against his stomach. He used his hold to turn her head so he could kiss her.

Wrapping his free hand around her waist, he found her clit, rubbing the small nub. She was soaking wet, making it easy to stroke the sensitive spot with so much speed, she came again within seconds.

"Motherfucker," she choked out as her body shook roughly.

Between the vibrator in her ass and her pussy's tight clench, Hank was a goner. He pushed her chest back down to the mattress, cupped her shoulders to hold her still and gave in to every desire, every need, every fucking impulse he had to fuck her until they both died.

He couldn't get enough of her. He never would.

Macie came once more. Or maybe her last climax was still going. Either way, it rang the death knell for Hank. His balls tightened and then he erupted, his cock pulsing as he came.

Macie's legs gave way mere seconds after the last drop filled her, and her body collapsed completely, leaving her facedown on the mattress.

Hank tugged the vibrator free without turning it off, loving the way it sent one more soft shudder through Macie's exhausted body.

Then he shut the thing off and tossed it onto the nightstand. Rummaging for the keys to the cuffs, he freed her hands. Macie remained lifeless through it all and he wondered if she'd fallen asleep.

As if on cue, Sally left her makeshift dog bed and walked over to his side of the bed, whining softly.

He chuckled as he picked the puppy up and placed her at the foot of the mattress. Content now that she was closer, the dog settled in, leaving no doubt she'd claimed that spot forever.

"You big softie," Macie mumbled, though she didn't lift her head to look at him.

Hank slid next to her, wrapping his arm around her waist as he kissed the back of her head. "How mad will it make you to know I'm hoping I put a couple strong swimmers inside you just now?"

He lifted his head just in time to see the corner of Macie's lips tip upward. "You're insane," she whispered, repeating the same sentiment she'd made earlier. "And you're taking me down with you."

"How so?"

"I'm sort of hoping one of the little guys breaks through as well. But I'm pretty sure that's the afterglow talking. Tomorrow, I'll be reasonable again."

"Let me know when that common sense kicks back in."

"Why?"

"I plan to fuck it out of you again."

Macie chuckled, then sighed. "Happy birthday, Hank Cooper."

He knew she was asleep the second after she'd spoken, so he didn't bother to reply.

Instead, he kissed her soft shoulder, glanced down at his adorable puppy and then lay there with a big-ass grin on his face until sleep claimed him as well.

Best birthday ever.

CHAPTER EIGHT

HANK STOPPED in the mudroom before entering the kitchen to wash his hands and face. It was a damn hot day, and his skin felt like it was carrying an inch of sweat and dust. He'd spent the better part of the morning working with a new horse, and he still had at least eight hours worth of chores left to do. He'd risen before Macie and waved to her from the paddock when she left a couple hours earlier.

It had been hard leaving the bed. She had looked so sweet this morning, her long brown hair a tangled mess on the pillow with Sally nestled up next to her. The puppy had actually dug her way under the covers, her head sharing the same pillow as Macie. His two girls. He'd snapped a picture of them with his cell and wouldn't admit—even to himself—how many times he had looked at it today.

A week had passed since his birthday, and Sally already had them both wrapped around her little paw. Macie had stirred at the sound of his camera clicking and rolled her eyes when she spotted the dog next to her. "You've already ruined her," she chastised.

He wasn't going to apologize for that. Or change. There wasn't a doubt in his mind he'd be even worse when kids started coming along.

He had to admit, Sally was stealing some of his thunder lately. Crawling in between them somewhere in the middle of each night. Macie was a cuddler when it came to sleeping. It could be a thousand degrees under the covers and she'd still be wrapped around him tighter than a coil. Not that he minded that a bit. Lately, though, it was Sally getting the snuggles.

Hank grinned when he recalled how cute she'd looked this morning when she left. Macie was all long limbs and soft curves—the perfect woman, in his opinion, though he knew she saw herself as too tall and too thick. She'd even said as much one night and he'd tied her up, keeping her on the edge of an orgasm he refused to give her until she promised to never say those words again.

Fucking media telling women they were only beautiful if they were stick figures. Annoyed the hell out of him.

He dried his hands and face. He'd have a quick sandwich and get back to it. Macie was working the late shift, so he'd be spending tonight at her place. While he didn't mind her apartment, he decided it was high time the woman moved to the ranch permanently. He had mentioned it to her last night, but she'd laughed and reminded him they'd only been dating six weeks.

He told her he'd sweeten the deal with a night-light, so it

wasn't so "unnaturally" dark. Hank had been sincere, but she'd only laughed again, thinking his words a joke.

He didn't understand why it should matter if they'd dated six weeks or six years. Hank had told her from the very beginning where he thought they were headed. His determination to get his ring on her finger had only grown. Macie was funny, sexy, smart, sweet—the whole package—and it was time to take things to the next level.

He'd broach the subject again tonight and this time, he wasn't taking no for an answer. It was silly for her to waste her hard-earned money paying rent on an apartment she only slept in a couple nights a week.

Besides, now there was Sally to consider, he thought with a grin.

Hank walked into the kitchen—and froze.

Blinking a couple times to make sure he was really seeing what he thought he was seeing.

"What the hell are you doing?" he asked.

Janice sat facing him, naked as the day she was born.

She laughed lightly. "I think that should be sort of obvious, Hank."

He narrowed his eyes at her use of his first name. That was Macie's to use. And only hers.

"Get up and get dressed, Janice." Hank struggled between pure fury and utter exhaustion. He was so over this shit. He had genuinely thought the woman had given up. She hadn't stepped foot on the ranch in over a month. Not since he'd told her Macie was his girlfriend. Porter had assured him he hadn't heard the last from her, but her absence had given him foolish hope.

"It's time for you to stop playing around, Hank. Time—"

"My name is Coop."

"Macie calls you Hank."

He wasn't sure how Janice knew that, but he figured at some point, the Maris grapevine must have been light on material so that little tidbit had made the rounds.

"That's right. *She* does. You don't."

He kept his gaze locked on her face, determined to make her see how fucking pissed off he was. "Get dressed now. And go home."

"I guess you think you're still sweet on Macie. Surely by now the bloom must be off that rose. She's all wrong for you. Sharon—"

"Sharon would have liked Macie. Hell, Sharon *did* like Macie."

Hank recalled the one and only conversation he and his wife had had about Macie nearly a decade earlier. They'd gone out to dinner at Sparks Barbeque. Macie had just started manning the bar, and she'd kept them in stitches the entire night with her silly stories. As they left, Sharon remarked that she wished she had Macie's energy and enthusiasm and how much fun it would be to be friends with her. He hadn't remembered that until just this minute.

"Hank—"

He took a step forward. His menacing look must have finally sunk in as Janice quickly corrected herself. "Coop. Can't you see that we're a better fit? I'd be a good wife. I'd cook and clean and..."

She stood slowly, and to Hank's horror, she leaned over the kitchen table. Facedown.

The same way he'd taken Macie the day Porter had walked in on them.

"And I'd welcome you—and Porter—into our bed."

There was no way in hell Sharon had told Janice about that. Best friends or not, Sharon had confided to him that she'd never told anyone about their foray into threesome sex —and Sharon didn't lie.

"How did you..."

"I saw you with Macie the other week. And I saw Porter standing there. If that's what you want, what you need, I can give it to you."

Hank's stomach lurched at the thought of Janice watching them.

"Get up from that table." His tone was deadly.

Janice's eyes widened and she started to straighten.

"What the *hell* are you doing?"

Hank turned to the doorway to find Macie standing there, taking in the scene and repeating his opening words almost verbatim. She didn't spare him a glance as she looked at Janice sprawled out facedown on his table.

His stomach lurched again, this time with pure panic and fear. God only knew what she thought she was seeing. "Macie—" he started.

Her gaze flew to his face as she lifted her hand to stop him. "No," she said. It was just one word, but a solid dismissal. She wasn't going to let him explain. Hank took a step toward her, but stopped when Macie turned back to Janice.

"Get your ass up from there, Janice. Dear God, what's *wrong* with you?"

Of all the responses he'd anticipated, Hank hadn't expected that one. "Macie," he started again, determined to set things right. He couldn't stand the thought that she might believe—even for one second—that he'd invited Janice here.

"Hank. You're gonna have to give me a minute to take care of this."

Janice had risen and was hastily trying to put her clothes back on. "Listen, Macie—" the woman began.

"No, *you* listen. I get it, I really do. You've lived your entire life wanting what your best friend had. Hank's a hell of a catch. So obviously when Sharon passed away, you started thinking you'd finally have a chance to grab some of that happiness for yourself."

"Macie—" Janice started again.

"Can you give me one good reason why I shouldn't kick your ass right now?"

With her dress back in place, Janice sagged back into her chair at the table, tears filling her eyes. "No. I can't."

Macie blew out an exasperated breath. "Shit. I guess this is what I get for forgetting my phone."

Hank glanced over at the counter and sure enough, there was Macie's cell. Typical.

"I really am sorry, Macie. It's just all those months after..." Janice swallowed, unable to speak Sharon's name, to mention her death. "He said he wasn't ready to date. Then I show up here and he's making *you* spaghetti."

Macie walked across the room and took a seat at the table. "Yeah. I know."

"You're just supposed to be his transition."

Macie grinned. "Sounds like we've been watching the same chick flicks. *When Harry met Sally*?"

Janice snorted and nodded. "I love that movie."

"Janice. This isn't the way to get a man's attention. You know that, right?"

Janice sniffled, wiping her eyes. "I didn't know what else to do. I thought maybe if I offered him..." Her words trailed off as she blushed.

"Sex?"

"Yeah."

"Hank isn't with me because of sex, Janice. Or," Macie flashed him a mischievous grin and quick wink, "at least, not *just* because of the sex."

Hank struggled not to laugh. Jesus. He'd woken up this morning one hundred percent certain he couldn't possibly love Macie any more than he did. She'd just proven him wrong.

"I can see that," Janice admitted. "I'm sorry I was such a bitch last week. Kind of hoped I could get you to move on when it was obvious Coop wasn't going to break things off."

"Last week?" Hank asked, but Macie waved him off again.

Macie sighed. "Yeah, well, it almost worked."

Janice winced. "When Betty said she overheard the two of you talking about wedding vows yesterday at the restaurant, I sort of panicked. Figured I had to make my move before it was too late."

Wedding vows?

Then Hank remembered. He'd been trying to help Macie

work on Amanda and Brandi's ceremony. The clock was ticking on the event and she was still struggling to write it.

"I'm in love with Hank, Janice. And I won't give him up without a fight."

Hank took a step closer to her. There would be no battle. Macie was the winner, hands down. Game over.

"No," Janice said. "It's not a contest I'm going to win. I can see that now. I'm just...I don't have your personality, Macie. I'm forty years old and I still live at home with my parents. I'm going to die an old maid."

"There are tons of single guys in Maris who would be lucky to date you."

Janice gave her a disbelieving look and shook her head.

"I'm serious. You just need some pointers on how to flirt." Macie pointed to Janice's ultra-conservative, plain dress. "And I caught a glimpse of your boobs. You definitely need to bring the girls out into the light of day. Catch their attention first with your smoking-hot tatas, then lure them in with clever conversation."

Hank wasn't sure he liked that Macie thought men were shallow enough to fall for that plan—and then he glanced at her tits and realized she was right. First thing he'd noticed about her had been her boobs. And then her laugh. While he still really liked her breasts, it was that infectious laugh that had kept him coming back for more.

Janice, however, appeared confused, which was not exactly an unusual state for the woman. Clever conversation was definitely going to be a stretch for her.

"Or you know," Macie said, when she realized her original plan needed some revision, "make them a home-cooked meal and bake them a pie."

Janice's face brightened. "I could do that."

"Tell you what, come by the restaurant one afternoon this week and we can put our heads together and come up with a list of eligible guys, make a game plan."

Janice laughed. "You'd really help me? Even after," Janice jerked her head toward Hank, "I threw myself at your boyfriend."

"Oh, it's fine. Honest. This only would have been a problem if he'd tried to catch the pass you were throwing. Then I would have had to kill both of you."

She and Macie laughed while Hank tried to decide exactly how serious Macie was.

The women solidified their date to foist Janice on some poor, unsuspecting Maris fella, and then Janice stood to leave. She hugged Macie and offered him a breezy goodbye as if they were passing acquaintances and she hadn't just been sprawled out across his table in her birthday suit.

"So...Janice, huh?" she said once Janice was gone, her voice laced with the same humor that was pretty much always there.

"What the hell just happened?"

"I was hoping you could tell *me*. Maybe fill in a few blanks."

"I think you already put most of the pieces together. I let things go too far."

"You think?"

He sighed. "She lost Sharon too. They were like sisters growing up. I got that, so when she stopped by several times a week, right after Sharon passed, I let her in. We ate dinner together, mourned together. Somewhere along the line, her feelings changed. Mine didn't. I tried to put some distance between us. I started going to Sparks for dinner, just to get out of the house and away from her."

"Did you tell her you weren't interested?"

The "are you kidding me?" look Hank flashed made her grin.

"Okay," Macie said. "Sorry. So you told her. And she kept coming around?"

"Yeah. Dropping off cakes and pies, inviting me out for picnics. When I couldn't convince her I wasn't interested, I avoided her. But the colder and more distant I got, the harder she tried."

"And when she saw you dating me, she realized you weren't still mourning Sharon. That you were ready for a girlfriend. I warned you that would happen."

She was right. She'd told him that the first night he asked her out. "When I told her you were my girlfriend, she looked almost happy about it, which I didn't get at the time."

"I was supposed to be the transition. The good-time girl. The one no man in his right mind would settle down with."

He narrowed his eyes. "I thought we established that you—"

Macie waved him off. "I'm not saying she was right. I'm just saying she did a number on me last week, which was only partly my fault, now that I know she had the hots for you. If you'd told me that, I would have understood her motives."

"If *you'd* told me she stopped by, and what she said, I could have laid it to rest right then."

"Touché." Then, because it was Macie, who liked to be right all the time, she added an adorable, "Asshole," to the end.

He sighed. "When I said I wasn't ready to date, Janice insisted when I was, she'd be right there waiting."

"Wow. That's sort of completely stalker-crazy scary."

Hank chuckled. "It didn't go quite that far. No dead rabbits in my kitchen."

Macie sobered. "No. Just a naked woman facedown on your table. Interesting choice of position on her part."

Hank had always admired Macie's cleverness. Now he wished she was a little less astute. "She saw us."

Macie blanched. "She saw you, me and Porter?"

"Yeah." Hank was as disturbed by that as Macie.

"Shit."

Hank watched her absorb that information. It only took her a few seconds and then, in true Macie fashion, she forgot about it and found another squirrel to focus on. "She thinks I'm too young for you."

Hank tilted his head curiously. "Part of that conversation last week?"

Macie nodded.

"Still don't understand why you didn't tell me she'd been here."

"She pushed the right buttons. I was feeling a bit sensitive about it. And then I felt dumb for letting her win."

"What did she say?"

"The same stuff a lot of folks are probably saying behind our backs. That we're a mismatch. That I'm not well suited to be a rancher's wife. As you know, my talents lie in making killer margaritas and gossip, not cooking or cleaning up horse shit."

"I like margaritas. And a good story."

Macie looked at him, her expression serious, pensive. "I think maybe I should reconsider my stance on moving in here. Apparently you're a hotter commodity than I thought. Better to stake my claim now than to have to keep fighting off the old maids."

Her eyes were pure mischief, and he laughed, loudly.

He decided the time was right. Walking to the spice cabinet, he pulled out the ring box he'd hidden there a week earlier. "You know," he teased, "I'm not sure just moving in is enough. It's like you said at the beginning. Open season on Hank Cooper."

Macie stared at his hand. "You had a ring box in your spice cabinet?"

"Figured that was the best hiding place in the house. No way you'd find it there."

"Hank," she whispered, when he got down on one knee.

"Seems to me your *safest* bet at keeping hold of me is to hop on a plane to Vegas with me."

She narrowed her eyes. "Vegas? Don't toy with me, Coop."

He opened the box, revealing the diamond he'd picked up in Douglas. He'd lied to her the night he'd gotten home for his birthday dinner. There had been no traffic jam on the highway. There was no way he could buy a ring in Maris and manage to get home with it before seventy-two people called to tell her about his purchase, so he'd stopped by a store in Douglas.

"Marry me, Whiskey Eyes." He took the ring from the box and slid it on her finger.

"Oh. Holy shit," she whispered, her gaze locked on her finger.

He rose, grasping her elbows to pull her up, as she continued to stare at the ring. "Say yes, Macie."

"Yes." Finally, her gaze lifted to his and she smiled.

He sealed the deal with a kiss. "I love you."

Macie cupped his cheek. "I love you too. I have to call the restaurant and tell Adele! And Sydney. And Jeannette. And—"

"I think I've caught the theme." Hank laughed. His first intention had been to drag her to bed, but he should have known hers would be to shout it from the rafters. She had a juicy bit of news to share. Apparently that trumped sex.

The fruit didn't fall far from that tree.

"You know, you don't have to tell everyone yourself. Just call your dad. TJ can take care of spreading the word for us." And then they could head straight to bed now.

Macie looked horrified by his suggestion. "You're right. If I tell him first, I won't get to tell anybody else. Come on. We'll go in person."

Hank chuckled. That backfired spectacularly. "Phone call won't suffice?"

She shook her head. "No. Besides, I'm supposed to close the place down tonight."

He tugged her hand when it was clear she was ready to leave. "Forgetting something?"

She frowned. "No. I don't think so."

He laughed and grabbed her cell from the counter.

"Oops," she murmured as she took it from him.

He let her drag him toward the driveway and his truck. Looked like the romantic lovemaking would have to wait until later.

And given Macie's excitement and ability to embellish any and every story, he figured it would be *much* later.

Hank was too happy to care.

She'd said yes.

CHAPTER NINE

MACIE STOOD at the window of her suite in the Bellagio, looking out at the bright lights of Vegas, and shook her head in wonder. One minute she was standing in the kitchen of Hank's ranch, looking down as the most amazing man on the planet proposed to her. The next she was surrounded by her family and friends at Sparks Barbeque, all of them hugging her, gushing over the ring, and then toasting them with bottle after bottle of wine...and beer...and then tequila.

Her head actually still hurt a little from that celebration, and it happened nearly a week ago.

Now she was standing in the fanciest hotel room she'd ever been in—the Bellagio was a far cry from the Super 8 she'd stayed in when she went to New Orleans with Amanda and Brandi a few years ago.

When Macie had described Las Vegas as her dream wedding location, she'd obviously envisioned something a lot tackier, cheesier and sillier than Hank had. The day after she'd accepted his proposal, she'd stayed in bed nursing the mother of all hangovers while Hank hit the Internet and started making arrangements. By the time she'd pulled herself out of bed late that afternoon, he'd booked their flights and this suite and made arrangements for an intimate ceremony in the hotel's gorgeous courtyard. Hank had even filled out the pre-application for their wedding license online.

Her mom and dad, Amanda, Brandi, Porter and Adele had all made the trip with them, insisting on being their witnesses. Porter was going to be the best man, Adele the maid of honor. And even though Porter and Adele had been carrying on with that bickering, somewhat-playful banter that screamed "Just fuck me already!" since getting on the plane in Texas, the trip had been a lot of fun.

Macie had tried to tell Hank she didn't need anything so fancy, that a quickie ceremony at one of the Elvis chapels or even a drive-thru wedding would suit her just fine, but he'd put his foot down. Told her she deserved to be surrounded by beauty at her wedding, which had been a challenge, since she'd stuck him with Vegas as the locale. He insisted he was going to spoil her with nothing but the best.

And apparently he'd meant it, considering there had been a limousine waiting to pick up the eight of them at the airport. The chauffeur had given them a scenic tour, driving them down the Strip and pointing out all the famous landmarks before dropping them off here.

No one had ever looked at her and thought "princess" before Hank. And given her less than girlie-girl ways, she couldn't really blame anyone. Now that she was here, she wanted to be treated like royalty all the damn time. Hell, she might look for a tiara to wear during the wedding ceremony. A woman could get used to this.

"Happy?" Hank asked, as he stepped behind her, wrapping his arms around her waist. In one hand, he had a single rose.

She took it, wondering where on earth he'd gotten it. The man was a master of surprises. "That word doesn't even touch what I'm feeling right now."

She saw his smile through their reflections in the window.

"Good."

She twisted to face him. "Hank, you really didn't—"

"Don't, Macie. Don't tell me one more time about what I did or didn't have to do. I know what you meant when you said you wanted a Vegas wedding. And as much as I want to give you what you want, I just think you deserve more."

"All of this is exactly what I would have wanted if I'd known to ask for it. I'm overwhelmed. And touched. And so fucking in love with you right now it almost hurts."

He swallowed heavily and though he didn't say anything, she could see the same emotions in his eyes. "I love you too."

He bent his head and kissed her. It was a soft melding of lips. Their tongues touched. Macie wrapped her arms around his neck as his hands moved along her back, pulling her closer as he caressed her. They kissed without heed of time. Macie had noticed that since she'd accepted his proposal, Hank no longer kissed her like his life depended on it. Now that they'd promised each other forever, they could relax, enjoy, develop their skills without fear of blinking to find the other gone.

It wasn't that the passion had faded. It had just blended

with commitment to form something even better, something Macie hadn't ever experienced.

Hank was the first to pull away. He glanced at the clock on the nightstand and grimaced. "Much as I'd like to move this to the bed, I told the others we'd meet them down in the bar in twenty minutes. I think they wanted to walk around the Strip, watch that dancing fountain outside and maybe find somewhere for a late dinner. You up for that?"

Macie hesitated. She was definitely anxious to see more of the city, but they had all day tomorrow for sightseeing, as well as a trip to the clerk's office. The wedding ceremony was scheduled for the day after tomorrow.

Hank noticed her delay in responding. "Macie?"

"Or," she suggested, "we could tell them to take off without us, order room service and eat really decadent food off each other's naked bodies. There's a whirlpool tub in the bathroom."

Hank's cell phone was in his hand before she'd even gotten to the tub information. "I'll call Porter. We can meet them for breakfast instead."

She laughed and reached for the room service menu as Hank explained to Porter that they were too tired from traveling to do much more tonight. Macie didn't doubt for a minute that Porter wasn't fooled by that line, but it was clear he didn't offer up much of a fuss.

"Okay?" she asked when Hank hung up.

"Yeah. Pretty sure he and your dad are going to give us shit for it tomorrow though. Porter was already making jokes about starting the honeymoon too early. In truth, I think he only would have been upset if Adele had bailed on dinner."

Macie agreed with that assessment. "Remind me to pull Adele aside tomorrow to ask her what the hell's going on with her and Porter."

"I will. And while you do that, I'll give Porter the third degree too. Maybe between the two of us, we'll manage to piece it out."

Macie handed Hank the menu and he called down to place their order. She was touched when he added a bottle of champagne to the list.

"You're a master at this romance stuff."

He shrugged. "Not really. I mean, I'm not doing anything that doesn't fall on the list, am I? Champagne, roses, limo, fancy hotel room. Pretty standard fare. In fact..." He slipped his phone onto the iHome and searched through his music. "I think soft music and dancing might be the only things we're missing. Want to practice our first dance?"

She nodded and stepped into his arms as Frank Sinatra filled the room. Macie laughed as he spun her around to "The Way You Look Tonight." It was the perfect song for the time and the place, with the big band sound, the old-timey feel, the lights of Vegas gleaming brightly beneath them.

Maybe it *was* textbook romance, but Macie didn't care. It was her first time taking the class and she loved every second of it.

The first song was followed by "Fly Me to the Moon," so they just kept dancing and spinning and laughing. They probably would have kept going all night if not for the knock on the door and the arrival of dinner. Hank tipped the waiter after he set the tray on the table.

During the meal, they discussed the ceremony. They'd

decided to exchange their own vows, so now, in addition to struggling to write Brandi and Amanda's ceremony, she was stressing out over finding her own words. "Why did I agree to this?"

"Isn't it usually the man who bitches about writing vows?" Hank teased. "Honestly, Whiskey. They don't have to be long."

"I guess you've already written yours."

He gave her a shit-eating grin. "Had them ready since the day after you said yes to my proposal."

"I hate you."

Hank covered up their empty dishes and picked up the New York cheesecake, nodding toward the bed. "Come on. You promised me food and naked body parts. We might be in Vegas, but I like the idea of licking New York off you."

* * *

Two days later, Hank stood next to Porter in the courtyard of the Bellagio in their Sunday best, surrounded by ornate beauty, flowers, music, soft sunshine and a warm afternoon breeze. None of it held a candle to Macie, as she walked toward him.

Two days after his proposal, Amanda and Brandi had shown up at the ranch and whisked Macie away for a full day of shopping in Douglas, the three of them determined to find the perfect wedding dress.

Macie had gone to great lengths to hide it from him since. She said she'd actually found it in a vintage shop, opting for something more old-fashioned. The full skirt came to just below her knee, and it had a high neck with tiny pearl beading around the neck and around the waist. It was cream, rather than white, which looked perfect against her pretty brown hair.

Amanda, Adele, and Macie's mom, Louise had arrived at their hotel room at the crack of dawn this morning, shooing him out and taking charge of Macie. He couldn't fault their efforts. Not one damn bit. Her long, wavy hair was pinned up in back with lots of curly wisps hanging around her face.

Macie wasn't usually one for much makeup, but she'd done something to accentuate her whiskey-colored eyes, making them look larger, deeper. Jesus. She was the most beautiful woman he'd ever seen in his life.

And she was going to be his wife.

When Macie reached him, she gave him an almost shy smile that betrayed her nervousness. While Hank had stood here before, for Macie, this was all new. Uncharted territory.

He gave her a quick wink that did the trick. Her grin grew, her confidence found in an instant.

"You take my breath away," he whispered.

Macie reached up and touched his bowtie. Once he'd revealed to Macie his plans for a fancy wedding rather than a ratty-blue-jeans, standing-before-Elvis affair, she had begged him to wear a tuxedo rather than his one good suit.

Her gaze slid along his body, taking him in from top to bottom. "Ditto."

Adele and Porter had taken their places next to them, while Amanda and Brandi sat in two chairs near one of the garden fountains. The officiant, a very nice older gentleman they'd met briefly yesterday, began the ceremony and then invited them to speak the vows they had written. They turned to face each other, clasping hands.

Macie went first. "Part of me can't believe I'm really standing here. The past couple of months have felt like a whirlwind. One minute I'm slogging drinks at the bar, the next I'm in your kitchen, drinking wine, eating spaghetti and falling in love so damn hard, I'm surprised I didn't get a concussion."

Hank chuckled.

"No one has ever looked at me the way you do, Hank." Macie's face sobered, her voice going softer than he'd ever heard it. "I've never looked into a person's eyes and felt such complete, such total love and acceptance. I'm loud and brash and opinionated. I talk too much about stupid stuff. You're the first man who has ever found all of that charming. You love me for all the things that make me who I am. I don't know how to say it, but even though we're getting married, I've never felt more free in my life."

He squeezed her hand. "I understand," he whispered. He wondered how many people in her past had told her to tone it down, suggested she might find a man if only she were a little less herself, a little calmer, quieter. She'd mentioned as much to him the night of their first date.

"I love you, Hank Cooper. And I don't care if people say we're going too fast or I'm too young for you or you're insane for marrying me. I promise to love you until the day I die, and I'll do everything in my power to make you happy."

Hank swallowed heavily, certain he'd never heard anything more perfect.

"I know it's been a whirlwind, Macie," he admitted. "I've been way too impatient to get to the next part, moving us along at the speed of light. The thing is, I've spent a lot of the last five years or so just holding on, living life one minute at a time, not daring to dream about the future. I took what I got and I was grateful for it. Grateful for every single second I got to keep Sharon. Seemed greedy to want—or expect—more. So I just took it one step at a time, moving so slowly, it was like I hadn't moved at all."

Macie wiped her eyes and nodded. Though Hank had professed to have written his vows quickly, the truth was, while the words had hit the page quickly he'd struggled with whether or not he should say them. He worried about talking about Sharon on his wedding day to Macie. Then he realized he wanted her to know, to understand, once and for all, why he was standing there with her. Why there was no other place on earth he wanted to be.

"You saved me, Macie. I don't think you realized it at the time. For months after Sharon died, I was drowning. In grief, bitterness, anger, loneliness. And then there was you. Inch by inch, you dragged me out of the murky depths. You pulled me up to shore and showed me a different way to live." He paused and gave her a grin. "So really, what it comes down to is this is all your fault."

Macie laughed, the sound mixed with a sob. "Figures."

"I look at you and I'm not seeing minutes or hours. I'm seeing years. I'm seeing a lifetime. I'm seeing everything I've always wanted, but didn't dare admit. I want it all. Kids and dogs and burned chicken and growing old and the sweet smell of bourbon. I want to dream about forever with you every single day, and I believe it exists. Believe that it's ours for the taking."

Macie had been fighting her tears until that point, but it seemed she'd given up the battle. She let them glide along her cheeks and he reached up to wipe them away.

Then he gave her the same promise she'd just made to him. "I love you, Whiskey. And I will until the day I die."

The rest of the ceremony—hell, the rest of the day—flashed by in the blink of an eye. They exchanged rings and kissed. They were engulfed in hugs and well wishes and tissues were passed around as all the women were crying and laughing at the same time.

They all went inside for a fancy dinner, followed by dancing and dessert and more than a few bottles of champagne. TJ had made one toast after the other, each one funnier and racier than the next.

And then, finally, he and Macie made their way back to the room, tipsy and giddy and more than ready to consummate the marriage.

Macie walked straight to the bed, glancing over her shoulder at him. "Undo my buttons?"

Her pretty wedding dress dipped low in the back, held in place by a dozen or so tiny pearl buttons that started halfway down her spine. He stepped behind her, slipping each one free as he kissed the side of her neck.

"Been waiting all day to get you here," he murmured.

She turned when the last button was unfastened. Macie slid the satiny material off her shoulders, the whole dress falling to the floor. She slipped off her heels as well.

Hank glanced down and enjoyed the view. Macie had

obviously bought a new bra and thong to go with her dress.

"Damn, Whiskey."

"See what happens when you give a girl time to prepare?"

He laughed at her joke. "Shaved legs?"

She nodded. "That's not the only thing I shaved."

His gaze flew to her panties as she toyed with the elastic. "Take them off, Macie."

Macie sighed, though she didn't sound upset by his demand. "Still lord of the manor? Even in Vegas?"

He nodded. It had become a running joke between them. The way she was always naked, him fully dressed. Hank wasn't sure why that was such a turn-on for him, but he didn't intend to change his ways anytime soon.

Macie tugged the thong down and then—because she was a quick learner and knew what request was coming next—she added the bra to the pile.

Hank took a deep breath and told himself to slow down. This was his wedding night. He wanted it to last, wanted it to be special.

Macie must have sensed his hesitance. "Hank?"

"Yeah?"

"We have forever."

Her words set him free. He gently pressed her back onto the bed and then, as she watched, he stripped out of his tux. Within minutes, he was on top of her, inside her, sliding in slowly, deeply, as she wrapped her legs around his waist, her hands around his neck, and kissed him.

Forever.

They had forever.

CHAPTER TEN

HANK STOOD at the end of the hallway waiting for Macie. Her cousin, Tyson, had offered up the use of his house for Amanda and Brandi's wedding ceremony. It was going to be a fairly small affair, with only about forty family members and close friends in attendance.

Tyson and Caleb had set up several rows of chairs by the lake with a rose-covered arbor at the front, serving as an altar of sorts. Meanwhile, Macie and her cousins had spent the better part of the morning decorating the tent and tables they'd rented for the reception with flowers and white tulle. As far as the weather went, it was a perfect day for a wedding. Not a cloud in the sky. Macie had been grinning from ear to ear all day, delighted for her friends.

And, he hoped, still reveling in their happiness. It had been two weeks since they'd said their vows and as far as Hank was concerned, the honeymoon could last forever. He was floating on cloud nine and had no plans to jump off the thing. Ever.

The wedding was set to begin in less than an hour. Macie had gone back to one of the bedrooms to check on the brides with Adele.

He was surprised when Adele came back to the living room without Macie.

"Where's Mace?" he asked.

Adele jerked her thumb behind her. "She must be more nervous than I thought. Either that or she's overly excited. She just darted into a bathroom. I think she's throwing up."

Hank frowned. Macie hadn't been nervous this morning. And being overly excited wasn't exactly a new thing for her. Which meant it was something else. "I'll go check on her."

Adele, clearly distracted with wedding prep, just nodded and darted toward the kitchen. "Cool."

Hank walked toward the bathroom, trying to get a handle on his sudden surge of emotions.

Two seconds ago, he'd thought himself the happiest man on the planet. That didn't even compare to what he was feeling right now.

He knocked on the door. "Macie."

He heard a muttered, "shit," and a brief, quiet cough.

"Just a minute, Hank," Macie called out.

Thirty seconds passed and he knocked again.

"Open the door, Whiskey."

He heard the toilet flush and the sound of running water. Finally, she unlocked the door. "Damn, Coop. Can't a girl take a minute or two alone to get pretty?"

He stepped inside, studying her face, his suspicions confirmed in the way she looked anywhere but at his eyes. "How far along are you?"

That caught her attention.

Her gaze connected with his, and she gave him an innocent look that didn't fool him for a minute. "I don't know what you're talking about."

"Did you take a test yet?" he persisted.

Macie narrowed her eyes. "You realize you're ruining everything."

He grinned, her words the admission he needed. "What was your plan?"

"I was going to put a pacifier around Sally's collar and see how long it took you to notice."

"Holy shit." A wave of pure joy crashed over him. He drew her into his arms, hugging her tightly. "You can do that next time."

She snorted. "There won't be a next time. I feel like dog crap. I'm not doing this again."

Hank kissed the top of her head. "Mmmhmmm," he said, knowing he'd convince her otherwise.

"I mean it, Hank."

"I know you do."

"You're happy, right? I mean, you said you wanted this. But damn, talk about a honeymoon baby. Or, more likely, a pre-honeymoon baby. Cause this probably happened before Vegas, now that I think about it." She was rambling.

He released her, surprised to find her nervous. "Macie. My God, baby. I can't even begin to tell you how happy I am right now. I never—" He had to clear his throat as his emotions started to clog it. The reality of what she'd just told him was truly setting in. "I never thought I'd get the chance to be a father."

Macie, astute as ever, noticed the impact her news had on him. She cupped his cheek and smiled softly. "You're going to be a great one."

Hank forced himself to take a couple deep breaths. Jesus. He was on the verge of blubbering like a fool. He needed to get his shit together.

"I love you, Macie." The words were simple. Words he'd said to her several times a day, every day, since the wedding. They weren't enough to cover what he felt right now, but they were all he had.

She reached up on tiptoe and kissed him. "I love you too."

"Are you're okay with this? Happy? I know I've been going on about it a lot. It's what you wanted too, right?

Macie rolled her eyes as if he'd just said something utterly ridiculous. "I know how to stop a pregnancy, Hank. When I realized I was late on my shot, I wasn't freaked out. Not even a little. I was actually sort of excited to think... well...you say you're not getting any younger, but neither am I. There's that clock-ticking thing."

Hank snorted. "You're only thirty-one, Whiskey. I'm pretty sure nothing's ticking yet."

"Maybe not, but I purposely didn't call Tyson to get another shot or the Pill. So really, when you think about it, I trapped you."

He laughed. "We trapped each other."

"Besides, if we're serious about a big family, we need to get started."

"Thought you weren't having another one?"

She lifted one shoulder casually. "I talk shit all the time. You know that."

"So you weren't kidding about wanting a big family?"

She nodded. "I'd love that more than I can say. Although I'm not sure what kind of mother I'd make. In addition to learning how to cook, I'm going to have to practice curbing my foul mouth. And God help us all when we're buried in dirty diapers and soiled bibs."

"I'll start looking for a housekeeper now. And we can get a swear jar. My language could do with a bit of cleaning up too. We got this, Mace. It'll be okay."

Macie wrapped her hands around his neck and he gave her a kiss on the cheek.

"I know," she said. "Feels like there's nothing I can't do now that we're together."

Leave it to Macie to find the right words. She'd hit the nail right on the head. With her, he felt invincible, powerful, ready to take on the world.

"You ready to go marry those girlfriends of yours?" he asked.

Macie glanced at her watch, then the open bathroom door. "You know we still have about half an hour, maybe more."

"You feel okay?"

"Comes and goes in waves. It just went."

Hank kicked the door closed with his foot, then reached out to throw the lock. "What's my time limit?"

She giggled. "Ten minutes. It'll take me twenty to put myself back to rights and stop blushing before I have to get up in front of my family."

"Ten minutes. Got it. Turn around, bend over that sink

and pull that dress up. I'll do my best not to mess up that pretty hair and makeup too much."

* * *

FORTY MINUTES LATER, Macie stood up in front of the people gathered and knew she hadn't made much headway on controlling her blush. Or her breathing.

With any luck, everyone would mistake her slowly fading arousal for nervousness. Adele had already perpetuated that idea by telling everyone and their uncle she'd thrown up earlier.

Macie brushed it off by lying about overindulging in wine last night. In truth, she hadn't had a drink since her suspicions about being pregnant were confirmed.

Only Tyson seemed to question the reason for the sickness. Which made sense, considering he was a doctor. She caught his eye and her dear cousin gave her a quick wink—either of support or as a gotcha. She had no idea which, but she was certain he'd pull her aside before the night was over and let her know.

When Harley, Tyson's girlfriend, began playing and singing the wedding song, Macie relaxed.

She'd been a nervous wreck about this for months, but now that the day was here, every anxiety disappeared and all she felt was happiness for her friends. The same joy they'd felt for her just two weeks earlier.

Harley sang "Sailboats," a Brooke Fraser number that was absolutely perfect for the moment. Her crisp, clear voice carried beautifully, accompanied by the gentle lapping of the lake as a soft breeze blew.

Though she was a terrible singer, Macie loved music and was always affected by it deeply. Amanda and Brandi couldn't have chosen a better song to walk down the aisle to.

The brides had had a rough go of it; after all, theirs wasn't a conventional relationship. For every person who embraced their love, there were three others who felt compelled to tell them why it was wrong.

Surrounded by so many people, Macie could see how touched the brides were by the obvious outpouring of support as they walked toward her. Amanda's face shone with pure love—an emotion Macie had only just recently come to understand herself.

She had been surprised when her friends asked her to serve as officiant nearly a year earlier. Part of her thought perhaps they were joking. But when they didn't crack a smile, when they began to list sincere reasons why they wanted her to do it, she knew the request was real. And because she loved them, because she admired their courage when it came to standing up to the naysayers and saying, "this is what I want, what I deserve," Macie knew she wanted to be the one standing there with them.

The music ended as Amanda and Brandi took their places in front of her and she took a deep breath. Writing the ceremony had been harder than she would have thought, and she actually hadn't finished putting the whole thing all together until she'd returned from her own wedding.

That was when she realized what her problem had been at the beginning. At the time, she'd been single. What did she know about love? What made her qualified to speak about forever?

Then Hank had asked her out and over the course of the last few months, the words she'd been struggling to find fell out. The rest of the ceremony came to her clearly the day after her own wedding in Vegas.

She glanced out at the crowd and found Hank staring at her. He gave her the thumbs-up and she smiled.

"Today is a celebration of love, friendship, commitment and family—those we were born into as well as those we've created on our own."

She looked out at the people assembled, quite a few of them members of her own family. She saw all the couples she'd watched fall in love and watched struggle to hold on, to overcome all those things that conspire to keep lovers apart.

"All of us here have our own love stories."

She saw Evan and Annie and recalled how hard they had tried to get pregnant, how it had almost destroyed their marriage. Then she caught a glimpse of Sydney and Chas holding hands in the third row, newlyweds themselves. The two of them had fought to stay together as Chas suffered PTSD upon returning from the Middle East. They sat next to Logan and Lacy, who were whispering and quietly chuckling at some private joke meant just for them.

"There's a quote that says, 'I saw that you were perfect, and so I loved you. Then I saw that you were not perfect, and I loved you even more.'"

Macie smiled when Tyson grinned at her. He was sitting with Harley—who'd taken her seat next to him—and Caleb, while her cousin, Jeannette, sat with her lovers Luc and Diego.

Tyson and Jeannette had faced down the folks in town who said three people couldn't love each other. They'd heard "it's not natural" far too many times and yet they hadn't given up, hadn't turned their backs on love and happiness.

Macie was proud to be a Sparks, proud to be a part of such an amazing family.

Amanda and Brandi held hands, looking at each other with such love, such happiness. Macie's heart was so full, she feared it would burst.

"Sure, there will be happy times, making dinner together, playing with your kitten,

binge-watching Netflix, game nights with friends. But maybe life won't always be great. If you can make it through the sad times, the mad times, the 'we're so freaking broke' times, at the other end, you're going to find yourselves sitting in matching recliners watching repeats of *Friends* for the millionth time and realizing there is no one else on the planet you'd rather do a whole lot of nothing with."

The brides laughed, as did the crowd. Their love of the old sitcom was well-known as they quoted lines from it constantly.

"You've chosen to be with someone who makes you think, makes you laugh, makes you better. Amanda and Brandi have written their own vows, which they'd like to exchange now."

As the brides shared their own promises and words of love, Macie lifted her gaze to Hank. He was looking at her as if the sun rose and set on her shoulders.

He made her think and laugh everyday. And he made her want to be a better a person.

Macie listened as her friends spoke and felt the tears she'd been struggling to hold in stream down her face. When the brides finished and looked at her, spotting her tears, the three of them laughed quietly at what sappy, happy idiots they were being. They exchanged the rings, all three of them constantly wiping their eyes and grinning their fool heads off.

Amanda had insisted on a champagne toast at the end of the ceremony, so Macie reached for the brides' glasses, handing them each one before claiming her own—she'd replaced her champagne with ginger ale. The guests had been given a glass of the bubbly before taking their seats.

Macie raised her glass. "Nikki Giovanni once said, 'We love because it's the only true adventure.' Brandi, Amanda, let the adventure begin. To you."

Everyone took a sip of champagne and then Macie said, "You may kiss your bride."

Harley, Caleb and Tyson had snuck to the back at some point and, at her cue, began playing "When the Right One Comes Along," by Nashville as the brides made their way back down the aisle hand in hand.

They were followed by the guests as they all headed to the large tent set up next to Tyson's house for the reception. Macie's mom and aunts had laid out one heck of a spread, the delicious smells of fried chicken and barbeque filling the air. It wasn't a Sparks' event without barbeque.

Macie's dad was hugging the brides, giving them both a kiss on the cheek, when Macie stepped under the tent. While Brandi's parents had come to the wedding, Amanda's family had refused. As such, Macie's dad was doing the first dance with Amanda, declaring she was "his girl" anyway. While Dad drove her crazy on most days, she loved him to the moon and back, and always would.

"That was incredible, Whiskey." Hank stepped up behind her, wrapping his arms around her waist. His hands gently stroked her stomach, and she knew he was imagining their baby growing inside. "You nailed it."

She twisted to face him. "I couldn't have written any of that without you. I've learned so much about love in the last couple of months."

"So have I."

Ty's Collective had already set up a small stage on one side of the tent, so once they plugged their instruments into the amps, the music began.

When Tyson and Harley started singing "Tenerife Sea," Hank took her hand and pulled her to the dance floor.

"When can we start telling people?" he murmured in her ear.

She laughed. "It's too soon."

Hank gave her a hesitant nod that set off her Spidey senses.

"Who did you tell?"

He gave her a grin that didn't look as guilty as it should. "Porter."

"Oh, thank God. I was afraid you were going to say my dad."

Hank snorted. "Give me a little credit. TJ is not someone I'd trust with a secret."

"But Porter is?" Then Macie rolled her eyes. "You know,

I was only away from you for the twenty minutes it took for the ceremony. That's pretty fast work. And you accuse *me* of being a shameless gossip."

"Couldn't help it. Sort of forgot to put my shields up. Sat down next to him, grinning from ear to ear, and he asked me what happened. It slipped out. But don't worry, I told him to keep it to himself. I just... Macie." He said her name with such wonder, such love, she had to hug him.

She couldn't be mad at him. Not for this. She was in the same boat, dying to scream the news to the world. And she knew what being a father meant to Hank, how much he wanted it, how he'd resigned himself for years to the fact that it wasn't going to happen.

But she knew it was smarter to wait until more time had passed. It was far too early in the pregnancy. Plus, it was Amanda and Brandi's day.

"No one else," she said. "Promise?"

He nodded. "I promise. But I'm pretty sure Tyson suspects something."

"I think he does too. I'll corner him later and swear him to secrecy."

They continued to dance as Macie chatted about the ceremony, what everyone was wearing, possible baby names, and wondering aloud if Porter would ask Adele to dance. So far, her sister and his ranch hand had avoided any discussion of each other, always dodging the subject whenever it was broached. The standard answer from both of them was the other was an annoyance and that was that.

Through it all, Hank simply listened, nodded and added the occasional yes or no answer.

She'd filled most of the next three songs with conversation before she caught herself. Grinning sheepishly, she murmured a quick, "Sorry."

Hank frowned. "For what?"

"Talking your ear off."

Hank gave her a quick kiss on the cheek. "Whiskey?"

"Yeah?"

"Keep talking."

ARE you ready to find out what's up with Adele and Porter? Their story, Waiting for Snow, is available now.

And be sure to check out other books in the Sparks in Texas series.

Waiting for Us (prequel)

Waiting for You

Waiting for Her

Waiting for Him

Waiting for Them

Waiting for Love

Waiting for Snow

ABOUT THE AUTHOR

Virginia native Mari Carr is a New York Times and USA TODAY bestseller of contemporary romance novels. With over two million copies of her books sold, Mari was the winner of the Romance Writers of America's Passionate Plume award for her novella, Erotic Research. She has over a hundred published works, including her popular Wild Irish and Compass books, along with the Trinity Masters series she writes with Lila Dubois.

Follow Mari:

www.maricarr.com

mari@maricarr.com